Somewhere This Way

Somewhere This Way
The Fiction Desk Anthology Series
Volume Thirteen

Edited by Rob Redman

The Fiction Desk

ISBN 9780992754792

The stories contained within this volume are works of fiction. Any
resemblence between people or businesses depicted in these stories
and those existing in the real world is entirely coincidental.

Please see our website for current contact
details and submissions information.

www.thefictiondesk.com

Printed and bound in the UK by Imprint Digital.

Contents

Introduction

Rob Redman

Our recent anthologies *And Nothing Remains* and *Separations* featured stories exploring loss, things breaking apart, and what comes afterwards.

These themes were suggested by the stories themselves, and by the cultural atmosphere of frustration, stagnation, and loss created by the ongoing Brexit saga, which cuts to the heart of the United Kingdom's cultural life and identity. The Fiction Desk doesn't generally take a political position, but as a publishing house that was planned in France, launched from Italy, and run first from England and then Scotland, we can't help but recognise the importance of a strong and open relationship between the countries of Europe (not to mention the benefits that come with freedom of movement).

Sooner or later though, it's necessary to take a look at where we are now, rediscover the pathways and the threads that we follow through life, and start moving forwards again.

The themes that sometimes appear in our anthologies aren't usually decided beforehand; as with past volumes, the ideas of path-finding and thread-following that recur throughout the current selection emerged as the book came together and the stories began to talk to each other. But it's only right that fiction should attempt to engage with the issues that affect our lives, whether by tackling them directly or simply by showing awareness of the cultural, social, and political context in which our stories take place. This is something we'll be encouraging in future anthologies.

The Fiction Desk will continue to welcome and showcase our usual selection of general fiction, but we will also be running a series of themed submission calls, encouraging our contributors to use short stories to explore a range of subjects relevant to modern life. The first call, for stories about different kinds of housing and the way they affect the lives of their occupants, is running this summer.

As change comes to our cultures, our nations, and the relationships between them, now more than ever we should be using the enormous, vital, and diverse energy of the international writing community to explore the way we live today, in the United Kingdom, in Europe, and around the world.

Alex Clark is making her fourth Fiction Desk appearance with this story, in which a pair of unusual threads become entwined.

Deep Green Leaves

Alex Clark

Mr Peabody was removing the last box of stock from his freezer when he heard the police arrive. He had been awaiting their appearance for some time, in the same way that a beach awaits the tide, or a tree the spring. At some point the expected event would occur, and until then, he simply went about his business. He laid the icy package carefully on a tea cloth on the counter, and sat in his chair.

Farid, in the ground floor flat, let them in. After a brief murmur of voices, their footsteps — light treads, unhurried — rose up the stairs, past Mr Peabody's door, and, after some fiddling with the lock, went into the flat above. Rosa's flat.

On Mr Peabody's table were a chopping board (green for vegetables), two carrots, an onion, and a knife. He took the knife in his hand and began to reduce the raw materials of his dinner into two-centimetre dice.

It was precisely twenty minutes after their arrival that two of the policemen came back down the stairs and paused outside his door. He could hear their voices. They rose and fell, came to a conclusion, and pressed his doorbell.

He placed the knife next to the vegetables, got up, washed his hands at the kitchen sink, and wiped them on an elderly but immaculately clean yellow-and-orange tea cloth, taking care to dry between every finger. Then he moved towards the door.

The police turned out to be one man — black, thin, middle-aged — and one woman, small, white, and plump. He invited them in. They declined chairs, leaning instead against the old Formica of his kitchen worktops. They looked around the room a lot, seeming surprised by its appearance. There was, in Mr Peabody's view, nothing remarkable about it. Brenda, who used to live downstairs, had once asked him if he didn't feel like he was 'living in a time warp'. It had something to do with the orange curtains. When they wore out, he said, he'd replace them. As it had turned out, Brenda had worn out first, and after that no one else came round. Apart from Rosa.

They asked him about Rosa: when he had last seen her, what she had said about leaving, whether she had had any visitors. 'Your landlord,' said the man, looking intently at Mr Peabody, 'says that Miss O'Neill gave notice two weeks ago, and he didn't see her or hear from her after that date. He became concerned about her. It appears that almost all of her belongings are gone. We need to find out where Miss O'Neill is, and to ensure that she is safe. You can help us by answering a few questions, if you don't mind.'

He didn't. He gave the responses he had rehearsed; carefully, deliberately, accurately. There would not be a problem, he knew, if he did not divert from the plan. It was a good plan. As he read out his answers he watched water droplets begin to form and run down the sides of the little box of stock on the counter, just visible behind the policewoman's left buttock.

They wrote everything down in a little notebook — the last time he had spoken to the police was so long ago that he had thought they might be using something more technological, but no — and then the woman said, 'Okay. To recap, you knew Rosa O'Neill as an acquaintance. A week ago she spoke to you in the hallway, mentioning that she disliked city life and was thinking of leaving. She seemed normal. You did not see her after that date, and you did not hear or see anything unusual in this house in the last week.'

'Yes,' he said. 'That is precisely correct.'

The policewoman gave him an odd look, then, but she closed her notebook and looked at the man.

'That's it, then,' he said. 'Thanks for your time.'

As they began to move, the woman knocked the plastic box with her hip, and looked round to see where the sudden sensation of dampness had come from. 'Oh,' she said, 'stock. My gran used to make that.' She frowned at it, as if it slightly offended her. 'What do you put in it? Chicken and vegetables and stuff, isn't it?'

'That kind of thing,' he said.

Then they were gone.

After he had chopped the rest of the carrot and onion, he went out onto his balcony and picked tomatoes. The block of flats had generous recessed white-stuccoed balconies on which Mr Peabody had found it possible to grow a surprising range of vegetables. Here, before the South London vista, he tended a contented thicket of green. It was all in the feed. He made it in an old red barrel, out amongst the plants, and he would give the recipe to no one. He had found long ago that people seemed to find it most acceptable if he shook his head and said it was an 'old boys' secret.'

He turned the spigot on the barrel and allowed a watering can to fill with rich brown liquid. As it did so, he took up a small sack of bonemeal which nestled beside the barrel, dipping his thin hands into the powdery contents and scattering a little over the soil around each plant. Returning for the watering can, he gave absolutely equal amounts of feed to all the tomatoes, and then he picked up his bowl of scarlet fruit and took them back inside with him. The colour, as he set them on his kitchen table, reminded him of Rosa's headscarf, and he sat down for a moment and thought of her.

She had announced herself, two weeks after moving in, by knocking on his door at two a.m. on a Monday. Mr Peabody slept very little, and had been sitting upright on his sofa reading *Vegetable Horticulture*, but nevertheless this took him aback a little.

The woman he found when he opened the door was tall, maybe in her late thirties, with a scarlet cloth wrapped around her head. Long, glossy, brown hair showed at its margins, the ends flicking out like feathers. The hand that was raised to the door was entwined with fine grey tattoo lines, like vines or ivy.

Mr Peabody found that most people, particularly anybody who had encountered him previously, tended to avoid his eye. This one looked him in the face with an unwavering dark gaze, said, 'I knew I was right,' and walked past him into his bare little home.

She was perched on the arm of his sofa by the time he got there, looking as comfortable as if she was on a cushion, examining the décor with interest. He stepped carefully around her feet, selected one of the two austere armchairs, and extended his hand out to her. She stretched over and shook it.

'Cold hands you've got there, Mr Peabody,' she said. 'But then they would be, wouldn't they?' She winked at him. He couldn't remember the last time anyone had winked at him. He was, for the first time in many, many years, at a loss.

'Got anything to drink?' she said.

At the back of one of the cupboards was an elderly bottle of peppermint schnapps, which had come with the flat. He chivvied the cap open and poured some into a small glass.

'Ta,' she said. 'I'd say I was sorry to be here so late, but I knew you were up.'

Mr Peabody frowned at her. He was absolutely certain that he made no noise moving around the flat. It was something he was good at.

'So, I thought: good neighbours and all that, let's go and say hello.'

'Hello, Gypsy Rosa,' he said.

She laughed, tucking her knees together and swinging her feet in their little brown boots. 'Ah, the doorbell label. It's a stage name, it's good for the fortune-teller trade. The only travelling my family did was to Lake Garda every summer. The gypsy thing's still popular, though, even with all the bullshit on TV about it. I hope my clients don't bother you.'

Mr Peabody had noticed that there seemed to be more people going up and down the stairs since Rosa moved in, but as they never knocked on his door it was of no importance.

'They come for readings,' Rosa said, sipping the schnapps and making a face. 'It's a good way of making money. I'm accurate, you see. Not many tellers are.'

She seemed to be waiting for him to say something, so he said, 'It's not safe to have strangers in your flat. Don't you have anyone to look after you?'

She looked sideways at him, and said, 'You've been around a while.'

'Thirty years,' he said.

'Really?'

'In the flat,' he clarified. 'Thirty years.'

She snorted, and said, 'I meant the whole time. Not just here.'

He thought, his body held completely still, his unremarkable face motionless. Eventually he said, as if it bothered him, 'A long time. I forget.'

She nodded, as if this was reasonable, and said, 'No. There's no one to look after me. I like it that way. The family I had were crap at looking after me anyway.'

'How did you know?' he said. 'About me.'

She looked at him over the rim of the glass, then leaned forward and put it down on the coffee table. 'When I said accurate, I meant accurate. The real deal. I know your look, Mr Peabody. When I saw you, I thought: he's passing for normal. The same as me. I know what you are but I don't think you cause too much trouble nowadays.'

He shook his head, mutely.

'No,' she said. 'Not much space in this modern world for wild things, now. It does its best to tame us.' She glanced around the orderly flat. 'I should think you have a nice, quiet life, you don't take any risks, and — if I had to hazard a guess — I'd say you set your sights a little lower these days. There was a dead fox on the road earlier, but it's not there now. I don't suppose you'd know about that, Mr Peabody?'

He looked straight back at her, and absolutely not anywhere else in the flat or its little kitchen.

'There's no need to be like that,' she said. 'I won't bother you. Not if you don't bother anyone, and I don't think you do.' She got up, elegantly, in one winding motion. 'It was good to meet you,' she said, holding out her hand again. 'We've got to stick together, Mr Peabody, us outcasts. Do visit any time.'

For some time after she had left, the smell of perfume haunted the flat. When he sat down on the left-hand sofa seat, the arm was still warm.

*

On Wednesday the police came round again, and were quite a lot less polite. He opened the door to hear the person on the other side break off in the middle of the phrase '*complete freak*', and found himself face to face with the woman from before, plus a much more serious-looking man.

They took fingerprints from him this time ('elimination prints'), and asked him more personal questions. The man tried to intimidate him, leaning his broad hands on the table and telling Mr Peabody that Rosa's absence was 'suspicious'. Mr Peabody looked at him and said nothing, which seemed to make him more aggressive, until eventually the woman took the policeman into the hallway and they had a whispered conversation in which he caught the words 'pointless', and 'probably Asperger's'. Then they went away again, after which he spent forty minutes getting the ink off his hands and disinfecting the table.

For dinner, he ate home-made steak and kidney pudding. Afterwards he waited until the house was dark and silent, took the key that the police did not know he had, and padded silently upstairs to Rosa's door.

He stood in the middle of the sleeping flat, and remembered her. There was little of her furniture left, but the massive, dollop-footed chaise longue was still there, reclining in the corner shadows. He moved over to it and slowly stretched himself out upon it. He lay, absolutely still, his arms folded neatly across his chest like the presentable deceased, and closed his eyes.

He remembered her bringing the chaise longue home. She had found it at Portobello Market, and had paid over three hundred pounds for it. It had a French pattern of birds singing from open-doored cages, in pastel colours. She had managed to talk the stallholder into driving it to her house in his van, but at the sight of the stairs the man's goodwill had evaporated, and he had left it lying half-in, half-out of the front door. Mr Peabody, drawn out by the noise, had been pressed into service to push the embroidered hulk up the stairs.

Once they got it into the flat, she had shaken his hand with theatrical emphasis.

'You're stronger than you look, Mr Peabody,' she had said, tapping his upper arm playfully. 'A useful creature to have around.'

Mr Peabody had never been flirted with in his life. It was an indecipherable feeling. He had moved his gaze to the walls, examining the pictures which covered them. They were all of birds. Birds sang from trees, under silver moons, flew from filigree branches.

She followed his gaze. 'Silly, I know,' she said. 'Real birds don't look like that. Real birds spend their whole lives avoiding getting eaten, or starving to death, or freezing.'

This seemed, from his long experience, to be a statement within a statement. He thought for a minute.

'Wild,' he said.

She smiled broadly, and wagged an emphatic finger at him as if he'd passed a test. 'Yes,' she said. 'You are precisely correct, Mr Peabody. Wild.'

He lay there, in the shadows and the silence, and tried to work out what he felt. In the end, he worked out that he missed Rosa. He missed her, and he wished she wasn't dead.

Before he left, he washed the bath again with bleach.

*

The third iteration of the police, which occurred on Saturday, involved him being arrested, put into a car and driven away. They shut him in a small, dingy room and told him that his fingerprints, which they had now checked, connected him to an unsolved offence. Officers were searching his flat as they spoke.

He said he didn't want a lawyer. They asked him a number of new questions, chiefly concerning what his prints were doing at the scene of a rather nasty crime in a north London mortuary. They were persistent, and were becoming irate by the time there was a rap on the door. After a muttered conference in the corridor, they all left and he was alone once more.

They brought him an unsatisfactory lunch. The meat in the sandwich tasted sad: thin and domesticated. He thought of the contents of his freezer at home, and wondered in a distant way whether the police would check it. He was so nearly finished.

They returned at the end of the afternoon, as the light was drawing in, and said he could go home. They obviously hadn't found anything at his flat, but they made it sound like a threat.

The flat was gloomy and cold. There were signs of minor disorder everywhere, where strange fingers had turned over his spare possessions. It didn't feel like his. For the first time he saw it from outside, as Rosa must have seen it: blank, functional, formed by routine. Not so different to the dingy room at the police station.

He switched the heating on, clicked on his lamps, and drew the curtains. Then he went back into the kitchen, opened the freezer, and took out the last of its contents. He placed it on the counter, sat on his chair, and looked at it.

*

She had come to his flat, for the last time, not three weeks ago. He had known from the bold, wood-battering rapping that it was her.

Instead of going to the sofa, as she usually did, she had gone straight into the kitchen and taken a chair. 'Do you mind if we sit here, Mr Peabody?' she said. 'This is business, and business needs a table, don't you think?'

He sat down opposite her. She placed her elbows on the table, and clasped her meshed hands under her chin as if praying. 'I did my cards tonight,' she said. 'They said the same thing they've been saying for the last five years.'

He waited for a while, then essayed, 'What was it?'

'I'm going to die,' she said simply.

'Everyone's going to die,' he said.

The corner of her mouth lifted, even in that serious face, and she moved her hands to cover it. 'I mean soon, Mr Peabody,' she said. 'Very soon.'

'Why?'

'Oh, one of those things.' she said. 'I don't think it'll be anything too awful. I'm not ill, and I don't see violence. It's hard to tell really. I just know it'll be quick, and I'll be at home.'

He looked at the table, then at her, then out of the window. 'Oh,' he said. 'Oh.'

She fixed him with her eyes: big, dark, sad. 'Are you upset, Mr Peabody?'

He took a small age, still and blank, to consider this. 'Yes,' he said eventually. 'I am.'

She rummaged in her bag and emerged with a tissue, on which she blew her nose quietly. When she had stashed it away, she said, 'I'm going to ask you for a favour. Because I think you still understand, even after all these years, about being wild.'

He nodded.

'I'm going to disappear,' she said. She looked upwards as she spoke, as if watching the flight of something far, far above her head. 'Like a bird, at the end. I want to fall from the sky and into the deep green leaves. I don't want *them* here, poking around my home, tutting at my things, putting my body in a nasty wooden box in their ghastly family crypt. Telling each other that I was mad, with my tarot cards and my tattoos and my vulgar ways.' Her eyes sparkled in the low light of the kitchen lamp. 'Ghouls,' she said. 'If you'll excuse the slight, Mr Peabody.'

He did. He listened as she outlined her request, and he agreed to it. There was no reason not to.

A few days later, at four in the morning, he was woken by an old instinct. Sitting up in the dark, he took a deep breath and scented a familiar, beguiling trace in the air. He took the key, let himself into her flat and carried out Rosa's final wishes.

'Everything,' she had said. 'All of me.'

*

As if in acknowledgement of the full circle turned, the final police manifestation came in the form of the two officers who had first knocked on his door. They were carefully courteous, and more than a little sheepish. They were very sorry, there had been an error with his prints. The crime which had provided a match was over sixty years old. Clearly he, Mr Peabody, a man of fifty-five, could not have committed it. It was extremely rare, but it appeared that he and the perpetrator had identical fingerprints. They could only offer their apologies.

Mr Peabody nodded, and took the letter of apology carefully between finger and thumb. He could feel them looking at him. 'And Rosa?' he said.

They didn't want to tell him, but they were worried. He could smell it on them. They were afraid of lawyers, and publicity. And so they gave him a little extra: there was no evidence of anything bad having happened to Rosa. She had sold her furniture herself, and paid all of her bills. The flat did not contain blood, or signs of violence. It was, if anything, remarkably well scrubbed and orderly.

'She was like that,' he said, being careful to look each of the officers in the eye. 'Tidy.'

As he showed them out he found Wadek, the landlord, manoeuvring Rosa's chaise longue out of the front door. The shape of it was making the process difficult. He seemed surprised at Mr Peabody's offer of help, but glad of it.

Once the chaise was placed on the pavement outside, the two of them stood for a moment and looked at it: Wadek breathing hard; Mr Peabody motionless, his wiry arms by his sides.

'What will happen to it, Mr Bartosz?'

Wadek rubbed his wrist where the chaise had trapped it against the wall. 'I thought I'd sell it,' he said, 'but no one wants to come and pick it up. So now I think I will leave it here. Someone will take it.'

*

It was around midnight when he heard the rain start. At first it pattered gently onto the plants on the balcony, then began to throw itself in small tapping bursts against the window. He thought of the chaise outside, imagined it standing proud in the gloom and wet. He flicked fretfully through his books, picking them out and putting them back. It was ludicrous to go out and look. It made no sense. Someone must have taken it.

Someone had not taken it. There was a carrier bag on the seat, lolling open to reveal a half-eaten takeaway in a polystyrene tray. The rain was blotting onto the fabric, onto the wings of singing birds and the doors of open cages.

'It won't fit,' he said.

*

It was hard, even for him, to get the thing back up the stairs. Every bump and scrape reverberated in the tiled stairwell. This was not in the plan. It was past midnight, everyone would be asleep, and he had no explanation – no good explanation, anyway – for being found dragging Rosa's old furniture into his flat. He was supposed to have no connection to her. It was stupid, stupid, but still he levered the thing round the stair returns and turned it sideways to finagle it through the front door of his flat and into the sitting room. It sat there, absurd and glorious in that spartan space, its little French birds filling the room with their silent song.

His own sofa was smaller, and much easier to carry down the stairs. As he left the shelter of the front porch and pushed it down the pavement, a slim shadow detached itself from the abandoned takeaway bag and trotted to the middle of the road.

It was a fox. It was young, lithe, alert. It paused in the middle of the empty carriageway to observe him, and he stopped and returned its gaze.

He had seen it before. It did not fear him. Once animals had known what he was, had skirted and avoided him, but that was long ago. He had become no more than human-shaped scenery, a creature of routine. At night they didn't move as he passed.

This time, though, it seemed wary. He picked out the glimmer of its eyes, fixed on his face. It was assessing him, as if it saw him anew. He wondered about taking a step towards it: maybe to see if it ran, maybe to see if it would come to meet him. But he couldn't quite bring himself to move, to lose the attention of those sharp yellow eyes; and so they stood for a long moment in the dark, the rain spangling their hair with diamonds, sharing the look that one wild thing gives another.

Poppy Toland took second place in last year's Newcomer Prize with this look at the way that mental health issues can entangle the threads of parental responsibility.

Our Gaff

Poppy Toland

Hollie and Adam had been in the same class for a few years apparently, but I never heard her mention him until the first term of Year Ten. She'd been passing a note to her best friend Anya, two or three seats away, when their new form teacher clocked her. The note was full of what I'll call *colourful* words about said teacher who'd been giving Hollie a hard time. There's no need to go into what she wrote, but it was offensive to say the least, even for an old potty mouth like myself, and well out of character for Hollie. The note had reached Adam, and just as the teacher was striding towards him, arm outstretched, Hollie sitting there bracing herself for the onslaught, Adam popped the scrunched-up note into his mouth.

'He chewed it a couple of times, then tipped back his head and swallowed it,' Hollie told me that evening. 'Told Ms Gregg I'd given him a biscuit. Such a safe bloke.'

At lunch she bought him a Yorkie from the vending machine, leaving it in his desk with a post-it saying *Dessert*. He looked over and gave her the kind of smile she couldn't describe without smiling herself.

'Who is this Adam anyway, poppet? And how come you've never talked about him before?'

'He's like you, half Chinese. I think people expect us to hang out and that's why I avoid him. Plus he's a bit of a loner.'

I was slightly miffed never to have heard of this half-Chinese boy. Hollie usually did a good job of keeping me up to date about what went on outside, never needing encouragement to witter on about who was best friends with who and who'd fallen out, who was being bullied by who, who was getting off or going out, who she had her eye on and, more and more over that last year, who had their eye on her. She'd become confident among her peers: not popular-popular, but with a solid group of friends, girls and boys, slightly offbeat kids most of them — obsessed by trip-hop music — but decent, and seemed to be generally liked and respected. And happy. And what more could you ask for, really? I had a sodding miserable time at school myself, so I appreciated her stories, got a blast knowing I'd single-handedly raised a girl everyone seemed to like.

*

It wasn't until spring term that I started to hear Adam's name again, coming up more regularly. He wasn't in her core group, but he hovered around it. They'd turned into proper teenagers by then. Hollie had a boyfriend, Neil. He was one of those lanky kids, impossibly long limbs that looked more like specialist building equipment than body parts, and dark lacklustre hair which would probably all be gone by his mid-thirties but for now flopped at the chin of his chiselled face, blinkering him, probably to blame for his extreme passivity. There'd been some serious shilly-shallying, endless whispery phone calls between Hollie and Anya, Hollie and Hayley, and I assume Hollie and Neil — although I never caught any of those — before they officially started going out around Christmas. In April, after a few serious talks with the pair of them, a deal was struck. They deliver my Labour fliers and get posters up around the ward for me, and I'd allow him to sleep over. They seemed solid, as solid as you can expect from a teenager like Neil. But he seemed genuinely committed and caring towards Hollie, and they were going to do it anyway — I figured it might as well be in a warm bed under my roof.

Word soon got out that I was a soft touch. 'Alright Hollie, reckon your mum would mind if we hang out round yours this Saturday?' she'd get asked on a weekly basis. Hanging out meant anything between six and twelve of them sitting around in Hollie's room, listening to their unsettling music at high volumes and smoking weed. Still, better than being outside loitering in streets or the park, risking arrest, or muggings or worse — like that poor French girl. Soon her friends were staying over.

Not all the parents were happy with this and Anya's in particular had a problem with how laid back I was and banned her from coming round. Hollie didn't seem as bothered as I thought, but hosting these weekend sleepovers had given her so much kudos she'd become like the sweetest flower, surrounded by the constant flutter of wings. And my god did that phone of ours ever stop ringing. I moaned to her, about the phone bill, about having a bunch of smelly teenagers in the flat all the time, and while it was a pain in the backside having to wait to use my own loo, I was chuffed that Hollie didn't seem a bit embarrassed about her old mum. Like my daughter I enjoyed being at the centre of the hub, got a kick out of spending Friday and Saturday nights on the sofa in front of the telly-box with a bottle of plonk and a takeaway, listening to the excited chirrup of voices, all that laughter, and the regular thuds — teenagers thud a lot. My only rules were that the kids had to come and say hi when they arrived and bye when they left; if they had weed, they roll me a spliff, and they brought their own food — no raiding my cupboards, that wasn't what the grocer's weekly delivery was for. Finally, those who were not staying over had to be gone by midnight, which was when I double locked and went to bed.

*

It was early May when Adam first showed up at ours. It was Eurovision night, mere days after our election triumph, and I was still dancing inside. Even though I couldn't get enough clips of our Blair looking dashing and impassioned as he gave his victory speech on the telly-box, that 'new dawn has broken' bit making me blub every time, it was still nice to have something new to get excited about.

'Eurovision, Hols! And we're in with a chance this year,' I said as the gang traipsed in from god knows where. It was to be a quiet gathering, relatively speaking, three girls and four boys, and I was hoping they'd sit down and watch it with me.

'No one gives a toss about Eurovision apart from poofs and lonely old women,' said Neil, walking into the room and making the whole place stink of feet.

This was the rapport we'd developed by then: a lot of banter and put-downs. I was just about to give him my worst, when I noticed the boy in a fluorescent yellow anorak standing apart from the group. I'd never seen his face before, but he looked exactly how I'd pictured from Hollie's stories.

'Not sure we've met,' I said.

'Hi Mrs Mann, I'm Adam.' He walked towards the sofa holding out a hand. He had an elegant face — rectangular, structured, with a thick thatch of dark bronze hair, out from which peered a pair of warm brown eyes.

'Ah, the note eater!' I said, taking his hand and receiving a surprisingly firm shake. 'And do me a favour, call me Jenny.'

'Jenny,' he said bobbing his head and giving an awkward grin. I watched a series of dimples ripple out from the left corner of his mouth, creating the pattern of a stone skimming a lake.

'I've been going out with Hollie all this time and never once has she told me to call her Jenny,' I heard Neil mutter as the group made their way through into my Hollie's bedroom.

'What a steaming pile of horse shit, when have you ever tried to call me Mrs Ma—'

'Mum!' Hollie feigned shock.

'Well it is.' I looked up and caught Adam's eye. 'You'll watch Eurovision with me, won't you, Adam pet?' I gave him a wink.

He held my gaze a moment and half smiled, no dimple this time, before strolling out after Hollie.

*

'He's an absolute gem, poppet, actually bothers to talk to your old mum. And he brought all the mugs to the sink before leaving, even offered to wash them. Adam's mum's Hakka Chinese, Hols, just like my turd of a father. Although he never got taught to speak it either.'

Hollie bristled. She hated the subject of fathers, hers or mine. It was Sunday morning — *the aftermath* as we sometimes called it. But she seemed bright-eyed and perky enough today. She'd strolled up the road with her mates at eleven when I'd turfed them out, returning with a brown paper bag filled with goodies — chocolate croissants, almond Danishes and what have you. We were both skint most of the time, but whenever she got any from her aunt, she'd share it with me and if I was ever lucky enough to get anything off her dad I'd do the same. Since last year, she'd even started to get served in the offie round the corner, despite her baby face, a cause for serious celebration. So we were sat on the sofa, her and me, noshing away while I had my little pry to find out more about this enigmatic Adam.

'Hey and Hols, Adam was telling me about his Saturday job at the rowing club. You could ask him to put in a word for you, nice and near if you're looking for a summer job.'

She shrugged, leaving her shoulders up by her ears as she continued to eat.

'Well even if you don't ... I might go along, wouldn't mind an eyeful of him flexing his biceps.'

Hollie gave a strong sigh. 'Mum.'

'Come on, Hols, he's dishy. And he's clearly got the hots for you. Why do you have to be so stuck on grouchy old Neil?'

She made huge disbelieving eyes at me. 'I'm with Neil, Mum,' she said at last, sounding small and offended. 'Do I ask you why you're so stuck on this old sofa?'

'I'm not stuck on it, it's just comfortable and I like it,' I said, hearing myself sound defensive.

'Well, that's how I feel about Neil,' she said, passing me the last Danish, scrunching up the paper bag and walking out the room.

*

Not long after, their GCSE mocks started and the weekend socialising ground to a halt. Hollie's never been very academic.

She's as dyslexic as they come, and she struggled with schoolwork. I couldn't help her other than to be there with her, doing a crossword or reading a mag as she tackled practice papers, reminding myself not to start chatting, and giving a flat-mouthed frown whenever I heard her sigh. It wasn't fair: all this school system did was make a girl like Hollie feel inadequate, when she had so many life skills to be celebrated and encouraged. I watched her chewing over a question, brow furrowed and jaw clenched, but as soon as she caught my eye she let all that go, her face breaking out into a bright smile. I marvelled at how I'd managed to produce this girl.

*

The Saturday after their exams, Hollie still seemed on edge. I hardly got a word out of her that morning, but put it down to anxiety about how she'd done. Their plan was to spend the afternoon playing rounders in Springfield Park before coming back here for a smoke. Hollie warned me they'd probably be a big group, but only five or six kids showed up. From the look of their eyes and their lurchy entry into the living room, I could see their rounders plan had given way to an afternoon-long boozing session.

'Alright, Jenny,' they mumbled, veering off towards Hollie's room. I got a proper look at her then, saw she was completely bladdered, her face pale, and only upright because Adam was keeping her so.

'Stone the crows, Hollie, what's happened to you?'

She shrugged and raised one eyebrow, a trick she could never do sober.

'She's drunk,' said Adam.

'I can bloody see that, Adam, I do have eyes. Has she eaten?'

'I got her some chips at the caff, but she threw them straight up.'

'Christ Hols, let's lie you down and get you something to eat. Everyone else, piss off home.'

'No mum, you can't ...' Hollie began, petering out as she realised that she in her current state was no match against me in mine.

Even though my legs were wobbling, I managed to rock forward to my feet. Adam rushed over to give a hand, but I shooed him away, saying I was just a bit lardy, not disabled.

'Neil! Get in here,' I yelled to the corridor of kids stumbling around putting on shoes. 'Where the hell's Neil?'

'He had something on,' Adam said.

'Leaving her like this?'

'He asked me to make sure she got home okay.'

I heard a snake-like hiss escape my mouth. 'Why the hell did you let her get into this state, Adam? I thought more of you.'

'I had a shift at the rowing club. Only got to the park at half four and she was already like this.'

Everyone left except Adam, who helped settle Hollie on the sofa. I could hear Hollie crying and Adam comforting her as I moved around the kitchen, my breathing made jagged by seeing my little Hols in such a mess. I just about managed to butter the toast, make a cup of milky tea and set them both on the tray without spilling, but felt too dizzy to carry it through and had to call Adam in to help. By the time I was back in the living room, I was feeling so rattled that all I could do was sit down, close my eyes and do those deep breaths I'd been taught. When I reopened them, Hollie was out for the count.

'So Adam, what the blazes happened?'

'I'm not completely sure, Jenny. You should probably wait 'til Hollie wakes up and ask her.'

I chased down his gaze, eventually locking eyes with him. I gave him a stern, none-of-this-nonsense look. 'It doesn't count as grassing, Adam. Hollie tells me everything.'

He sighed, looked about to say something, but then shook his head.

'I'm taking it's got to do with Neil?' I asked, reaching for the toast.

He nodded.

'Have they broken up?'

'Yeah, seems so.'

'I'll ring his fucking neck, I'll —'

Adam gave a pronounced blink, cutting me off.

I turned on *Stars in their Eyes*, feeling dissatisfied and frustrated. We watched telly, exchanging small talk about what was on the screen, until Hollie woke up and asked us to help her get to bed.

*

Hollie was in a terrible way the next day, and not just from her hangover. Adam had gone back home the night before — his parents didn't let him stay out — but was back bright and early the next morning. The three of us took turns making tea and sat there as Hollie told and retold the story.

Neil had dumped her for a girl in the year above. It just wasn't working, he'd told her on the phone the night before her last exams. I was already so against him, that's why she'd hidden it. She thought they'd get back together and so it would be easier if I didn't know. She put the break-up down to the fact they hadn't seen each other much during the exam period. But then on Saturday he'd shown up with Amber.

'They were all over each other, Mum, all over,' she said, doing a hideous impression of tongues and hands, before grabbing her head and moaning as she lay back down on the carpet.

'What a piece of shit! If he comes anywhere near here again I'll rip his —'

'Mum!'

'Rip his jeans even more than they are already, was what I'd've said if you'd let me finish!'

Hollie groaned and Adam's eyes crinkled. He'd brought round a Frisbee of all things, and was trying to coax Hollie out into the sunshine. She gave a bark of laughter at the suggestion — she was too hung-over, and like fuck she was ever going back to Springfield Park. I could tell that having Adam there was making her feel better though, and thought maybe she'd get through this without too much suffering. But as soon as he left, her mood plummeted. She went to bed early, asleep I assumed, until turning off the telly to go to bed I heard her sobbing. I went through to her room and crouched down beside her bed, but she didn't look up, not even when my knees gave off a loud crack. I stroked her hair and tried to hug her, but she wriggled to the wall side of the bed. 'Sorry Mum, I just want to be on my own.'

I dragged myself to my own bed and lay there, listening to the sound of her crying, while I cried myself to sleep too.

*

I let her have Monday off school. She stayed in her room for most of it, listening to 'Unfinished Sympathy' on repeat. *Blue Lines* was an album I knew only too well. It was the soundtrack of Hollie's teenage years, and this song had just found a definite place in her story. She didn't want me to comfort her — she didn't want me at all. 'I'll just be on the sofa, poppet,' I said each time I shuffled in to check on her, and she'd nod and push her face back down into the pillow, that eerie melody still gushing out from her stereo, making me feel nauseous with its talk of souls without minds stuck in bodies without hearts. I hated it, but I couldn't ask her to turn it off.

The next day I was surprised to hear her getting up and showering, packing her school bag. She came through to my room with my morning cup of tea and set it on my bedside table, all breezy.

'Mum, can you do this for me?' She rested a pad of letter paper on a pile of my library books and laid it out in front of me, handing me a biro.

'Are you sure you're alright for school?'

She nodded.

'You're ready to see Neil? I mean, another day or two off won't hurt.'

'I'm fine,' she said, standing over while I wrote the sick note. She took it off me when I was done, folded it and popped it in an envelope addressed to Ms Gregg. She hardly needed me anymore. She arranged my books back on my bedside table, and if she noticed the pile of balled up hankies there, she didn't mention them. She handed me my tea, gave me a peck on the forehead and she was gone.

*

Hollie messed up royally on her exams, only passing French and RE and those by a whisker. A letter arrived in the post from Ms Gregg saying she understood that I had a psychological condition that made it hard for me to leave the house, but she thought it was imperative we met to discuss Hollie's future and she'd be willing to come to the house if that helped. *Psychological condition ...* What was this lady, a doctor now? *Imperative ... willing to come to the house ...* Such jumped-up language. I tucked the note inside my Danielle Steel, meaning to respond when I could muster the energy, but then Hollie ended up taking the book back to the library without realising there was a note between its pages, and I thought, well, that's a sign really. It kept me awake at night sometimes, the fact that I hadn't written back, but by that point it was almost the end of term and I was certain Ms Gregg would be too busy, and then it was summer holidays.

*

The gatherings had stopped along with Neil's disappearance from our lives, but Hollie didn't seem to mind. Somehow Adam managed to get her enthused about the great outdoors – she hadn't inherited any genes for that kind of pursuit, not from her dad and certainly not from me. Adam never came round any more; she only ever saw him outside. He got her into rowing and she was up early each morning all through the summer holidays, down at the club, cleaning equipment and tidying in exchange for use of the boats. They spent the afternoons cycling around, playing tennis, walking Adam's dog Chutney along the Lea, Frisbee, picnics, you name it. I hardly saw her and when I did I barely recognised her. A different girl had emerged: one who was lean from all the exercise, bronzed from so much time spent outside, and who seemed confident in a quiet, adult, but far less *Hollie* way than before.

What was going on with her and Adam? I asked once. Were they friends or more? She just shrugged. It didn't need a label, they just hung out and made each other happy, she said. Would she ever want him to stay over? She shook her head. Sleeping with Neil so soon had been a mistake. Adam and his family were more traditional. The two of them were exploring things in a different way. Fair enough, I nodded. Well, would she ever like him to spend an evening round at ours in that case; I could give them the dosh to choose a video from Blockbuster and order us all in a Dominos? She smiled and said that sounded nice. But it never happened. I brought it up a couple more times and then let it go.

He bought tickets for Massive Attack, playing in Finsbury Park on second August. I was gutted. For the first time since she was born, I didn't spend my birthday with her. I barely left my bed anymore. Hollie helped move the telly-box through to my bedroom, and found me a little table that went over my legs so I could have my meals there. She'd sometimes sit with me in bed, but never for very long – she always had somewhere to be. She'd try and open the curtains, let in the sunlight, but I told her I preferred them closed. I heard her on the phone to the council once, discussing my situation and saying how I needed assistance. Soon I was getting Meals on Wheels, and a carer called Cynthia who visited twice a week to bathe me, cut my nails and such like. It wasn't like I wanted Hollie to be doing that degrading stuff for me, but I hated the feeling of being palmed off.

It all came to a head on the last Sunday of August, two days before Hollie was due back at school. I turned on the telly and with what felt like a punch in the belly, discovered that everything had changed. I hadn't realised she meant so much to me, but seeing the banner across the telly, *Princess Diana Dead*, I found myself unable to breathe. Hollie came in and perched on the bed, and we held hands as we watched the BBC reports in silence, images of that mangled car and the remains of the pillar it smashed into. We sat there for god knows how long, in a state of near-hypnosis, trying to process that information being relayed again and again. Dangling over a cliff, it was only Hollie's hand keeping me from plummeting.

'Tea?' she said eventually.

I nodded and she wriggled her hand out from mine, shaking it out.

She handed me my cup and asked if there was anything else I needed before she went out.

'Excuse me?'

'I'm meeting Adam, Mum. We've got a court booked.'

I gave her a look.

'What?' she said, her voice hardened.

'It's a day of national mourning, Hollie. I'm in shock and I need you here.'

I saw her bite her lip, look from the clock, to the bed, to the clock. 'I'm really sorry Mum, I've got to go – he'll be waiting.'

'But I'm your mum.'

'I'm sorry.' She turned to leave.

'Hollie ... Please.'

She turned around. 'I'll be back this evening,' she said, more pity in her voice than love.

I was sobbing loudly before she was out the door, but she didn't change her mind, she didn't even say goodbye.

I needed something to take my mind away from the gloom, but flicking through telly channels all I found was Diana footage or static images of the Union Jack with 'God Save the Queen' playing on a loop.

I felt a rare surge of energy, an urge to do something, take control. I wiggled my hips back, gradually working my way up the bed until I was sitting upright. I closed my eyes and pictured myself getting up, pulling on my tracksuit, opening the front door and walking outside. Feeling the sunshine on my cheeks, a slight breeze against my ear. Maybe hearing a bird. It didn't need to be very far, just down the path past our block, I wouldn't even have to go out the estate. Just take the first step, Hollie always said. I imagined how proud she'd be when I told her.

Instead I found myself bashing my head against the wall, again and again. I carried on, harder each time, tears jerking from my closed eyes, until the physical pain overpowered all the other pains but still I kept going. I was certain I'd made a dent in the wall, filled it with a bloody gooey mess of brains and splintered skull, but when I eventually stopped and opened my eyes, the wall was spotless, the room just the same as before, Diana's wrecked car still on the telly screen.

*

I was taken into a care home not long after, where I am to this day. Hollie moved in with Adam and his family. She left school with two GCSEs and took a receptionist job, while Adam continued his schooling. She fell pregnant in his last year at school and the council found them a flat in the area. They have two little girls now, Esther, three, and Fern six months, little poppets the pair of them, just like miniature Hollies.

Just before Fern was born they decided to get married, and of course, I said I'd be there. For a bit, I really thought I could be. Evelyn, the staff nurse here, ever such a sweetheart, even went out and got me a smart purple M&S skirt-suit from SCOPE to wear for the occasion and said she'd arrange for her friend Betty to come in and do my hair. But on the day I couldn't, I just couldn't. I would have worried about disappointing Hollie, but to be honest I think it had gone past that.

Hollie comes to visit three times a week, but never stays long and I can tell that it's a bit of a duty. She only brings Fern now, says it's because Esther's at playgroup, but I don't think that's the whole story – she stopped bringing Esther once the little thing started questions like why so many people lived in my house and why I was always in bed. I don't blame her, I wouldn't have wanted Hollie around all these headcases when she was Esther's age either. Adam never visits, and I think I know why. Of course, it could have been Hollie who got me sectioned, but I'm sure he'd have had a hand in it. Either way, I try not to think about it too much.

I had a flash of inspiration the other day, and handing Evelyn a twenty, asked if she'd do us a favour and pop by Woolies or Our Price in her lunch break and pick me up the album *Blue Lines* by Massive Attack. She said she'd see what she could do. It took her a couple of days, but eventually she came back looking jolly, and handed me the CD and my change. I placed it inside the Discman Hollie gave me to listen to talking books on, and arranged my hair so the spongy bits of the headphones fitted right over my ears. I asked Evelyn if she could lay me out flat, holding off while she fussed around, plumping up pillows and whatnot. Only when she was finally out of the room did I press play.

*

I never told Hollie how much this music used to scare me, all those beats and clatters and clicking and scratching, far too much going on at once, and that haunting woman's voice floating over it all. But lying here, listening to it with closed eyes, as I start feeling that deep dread closing in on me, making my hair stand on end, I finally get it. That's the point – you're meant to let it creep in and take you. I submit, allowing the beat to carry my body up off the bed, while the different rhythms lap over me, dissolving layers away from me, nibbling at my edges, filling the empty spaces, so that when the woman starts singing my chest is ready to be forced open and my heart to burst out. And for a moment I'm back home with her, sitting on the sofa like sisters with the thick grey woollen throw covering both of us. We've got the telly on, but we're not really watching, we're just chatting and laughing, cracking each other up. It's so real that I can even smell her, a mixture of digestives and white musk and that earthy cinnamony scent of her skin.

The CD finishes. I take off the headphones and put it all back on the bedside table. I look across the bars of my hospital bed, past the half-wilted pink tulips she brought me last week, and count out how many full turns the short hand needs to make before I'll see her again.

Some roads are more literal than others, as in this story from Michael Hurst. Like Alex Clark, Michael is based in Cheltenham.

Life on the Road

Michael Hurst

'You didn't get me a coffee?' says Terri, when Richard returns from paying for the petrol.

'There was a queue.'

Richard drives out of the forecourt, along narrow utility roads, and past a coach park to rejoin the motorway. Terri hunts through her handbag. She pulls out a few CDs and puts them in the glove compartment. The early sun rises over a long strip of hills. She yawns and wonders where they are. They make this trip to head office every month. She has no idea what lies away from the familiar route. It takes her a second to think what county they're in: Oxfordshire, Buckinghamshire? Something like that.

'What are those hills?' she says.

'Dunno. Chilterns, maybe?'

She pauses. 'This is a big difference between you and me, you know.'

'What is? The Chilterns? It might not be them. Christ knows.'

'No. The petrol. Do you know, I've never used a service station?'

He looks incredulous.

'Really. Not once. It's so much more expensive.'

'Don't you ever forget to fuel up before a trip?'

'If I do, I go out specially. The night before.'

'Well ... good for you.'

*

They leave the motorway at the next junction and after an hour they pull over at a lay-by. Richard wanders in circles on the tarmac. Terri stretches. Richard seems to want his own space and she leaves him to it. When the time comes they swap seats. Richard holds out the key to the Alfa Romeo with his head bowed. Terri gets in first and quickly slides the seat back. She doesn't like to draw attention to the difference in their heights.

At a roundabout, a white van presses forward at the next lane entrance, the driver willing Terri to let him out even though she has right of way. Terri pushes on regardless and the van driver slaps his mobile phone on the steering wheel and hunches over it, avoiding eye contact. Two other builders are squashed into the cab next to him, seated in age order, the driver the eldest and on the far side a young lad. They're laughing at something the driver has said, the young lad showing his teeth in an endearing way.

'When do we ever laugh like that?' says Terri. 'Not just you and me, but anyone?'

'He's probably telling some rape joke,' says Richard.

'If he is, it looks like a good one.'

She accelerates away from the roundabout, leaving the van far behind.

The radio switches to adverts.

'Put on one of my CDs,' says Terri. 'You choose.'

Richard opens the glove compartment. He starts checking the CDs, swapping the discs from case to case.

'Why do you put them in the wrong cases? Why would anyone do that?'

He holds up two CDs. One is Bob Dylan's *Bringing It All Back Home*. The other is a compilation of nineteen-eighties pop songs.

He reads from the track listing: 'Mel and Kim, Bryan Adams, Bananarama.' He turns over the case as though hoping to find something better, then turns it back. 'Here's a dilemma. The best travel music is cheese. But driving is one of the most dangerous things we do. And when the car is upside down and you're lying semi-conscious, waiting for the firemen to cut you out, do you really want to be listening to Chesney Hawkes?'

He makes to take out the Bob Dylan.

'Put on the cheese,' says Terri. 'I'll take my chances with the firemen.'

'Watch out!' says Richard. They have driven over a small gradient, and ahead the traffic has come to a standstill. A Volvo in front applies its hazards, and Terri brakes heavily. The Volvo and the cars in the adjacent lanes seem to race towards them in a flood of red brake lights. They manage to stop in time, and then comes the tense moment as they wonder whether the cars behind them will do the same.

A far-reaching view of the dual carriageway stretches ahead as the road curves to the left and then climbs another hill. There are thousands of stationary cars.

'That is a depressing sight,' says Richard. He slides in the eighties CD and Paul Hardcastle's '19' starts to play, too loudly, still at the volume for full speed driving. 'And that is a depressing sound,' he says, turning it right down.

From their vantage point they can see drivers further along getting out of their cars, chatting to each other and peering down the road.

Richard is already slapping his hand against the door. 'I think they've closed the road,' he says. He reaches to the back seat and rummages in his bag until he finds a can of Diet Coke, which he opens and places in the extendable drinks holder above the stereo.

'It'll make you wee,' says Terri. 'You'd better phone Sally and say we're going to be seriously late.' She tends to be philosophical about traffic jams: if you can't change it, no point getting upset about it.

Richard rests his jaw in his hands and leans away from her, staring at the rows of vehicles to his left. Terri takes up a mirror-image pose, looking out at the central reservation. It consists of a surprisingly varied jumble of vegetation. Wide clumps of yellow flowers — she searches her mind for what they might be: wild parsnip? — are interspersed with white cow parsley. The sun is now higher in the sky but is being obscured by thickening dark clouds. A kestrel hovers above the neighbouring fields. Its wings, almost horizontal, seem too wide for its body. She watches the bird stabilising with occasional rapid wingbeats until it spots its prey and swoops down.

A few fat drops of rain land on the windscreen and soon it's pouring down. Terri leaves the wipers off. The central reservation and surrounding cars distort into prismatic smudges.

After thirty minutes they hear a faint siren. The sound is persistent and gets gradually louder. All around them, drivers restart their engines as though glad of the opportunity to have something to do. The cars in the outside lane move into the narrow run-off area that borders the central reservation. Terri does the same, the tyres producing a spitting sound as they throw up loose gravel.

An ambulance streaks through the gap they have created, sirens at full blast, its wheels sending a hissing wave of water from the road. The car rocks as it passes. It takes several minutes for the ambulance's blue lights to cut through the traffic ahead.

'If you were a pedestrian, would you rather be hit by a car or an ambulance?' says Richard.

'That's a cheerful question. A car.'

'Explain.'

It's something they do, Terri and Richard, these hypotheticals, but Richard's voice is flat. She tries to muster her usual breezy response.

'If you were run over by an ambulance, you would get immediate medical care of the highest quality. But ... it would be like a brick wall hit you and you'd probably die.'

'With a car you could go over the top and land on your head. You could be waiting twenty, thirty minutes for assistance. Worse, an unskilled member of the public might try to help. You could end up with needless spinal injuries.'

'You're in a funny mood today.'

Richard swigs his Diet Coke and places it back in the drinks holder. 'I need a wee,' he says.

Terri doesn't reply.

Richard starts fidgeting. He makes furtive glances through his window, then opens the door and gets out.

She watches him hurry across the lanes, between the stationary vehicles. Richard's body is lean and tight like his face. His crimson Joules gilet clings to his torso. Terri smiles. He has a different coat for every micro variation in temperature. Soon he reaches the cab of a box truck and disappears behind it.

He returns to the car with a more measured walk, despite the rain, glancing around at the vehicles with a defiant expression. And before long four, five, six drivers leave their cars to do the same thing.

'I've started a trend,' says Richard.

It's another half hour before the dual carriageway is reopened and they can move again. By the time they reach the accident site, the police have cleared away most of the damage and then the traffic returns to its normal speed.

Terri stays in the fast lane and accelerates. Unwilling to talk, she turns up the pop CD and the music fills the car. Richard stares out of the opposite window. The Alfa Romeo seems sluggish. She drives at eighty miles an hour but it requires a continual effort on the pedal to maintain the speed.

She tries to ignore Richard's turned-away head. It surprises her that she wants to cry. The only way to stop it is to focus on the road, tapping her hand on the steering wheel in time to the music. Memories of conversations with Richard keep coming back to her. They first met on a team-building event, a beautiful summer's day at a lake where they had to build rafts from plastic barrels. They went for a walk in some woods and Richard pointed out the tree trunks, which were covered in a green fur. 'That's a good sign,' he said. 'Lichen growing on trees means there's no pollution in the air.' She'd been impressed that a guy from the office would know things like that about nature.

Something's odd about the car. There doesn't seem to be much of a gradient on the road, yet she has the accelerator pedal on the floor. A metallic rattle starts up. It's coming from Richard's Coke can in the drinks holder.

Richard looks over at her. 'What the hell's going on?' he says.

The can is juddering wildly.

'There's *smoke* outside.'

Terri looks out of the window and sees the smoke.

'Puncture,' she says.

They are coming up to a major roundabout, where the dual carriageway joins the next motorway. It's the last place you'd want a puncture. The traffic is slowing, ahead of a short queue. She indicates, and muscles her way into the nearside lane.

'I think there's a service exit just before the roundabout,' says Richard, leaning from his seat to peer forwards.

Sure enough they are approaching a small exit, with a tiny sign that reads 'Depot'. She's never noticed the exit before but is glad to pull into it now. The lane is a dead end that leads at once to a mini-roundabout. Three utility yards fan off via metal gates and security intercoms. The biggest yard is full of police vehicles.

There's nowhere obvious to park and Terri stops on the roundabout between two of the yard entrances. The storm has calmed and left a steady fine rain. They wait for a moment, watching the dismal view through the wipers. Then they unbuckle their belts and leave the car at the same time.

The front driver-side tyre is flat, and acrid smoke pours from it.

'How fast were you driving?' says Richard.

'I don't want to think about it.' Terri opens the back door to pull out a big blue coat.

'Didn't you notice?' He points to the smoke and the tyre. 'This?'

'Didn't you?'

She pulls out her mobile phone and waves it in his face to stop him talking. The recovery number is saved in the phone. She's organised like that.

'At least we can wait in the car, parked here,' she says, when she's finished with the call.

'How long do they say it'll be?'

'Up to an hour. From now.'

Richard strides around the car and opens his door, slamming it after him. Terri sighs and gets in out of the rain.

A small van comes out of the depot, followed by a police car. The van climbs the curb and parks on the pedestrian pavement in a fast, neat manoeuvre. A policewoman gets out of the car. She stands in the drizzle and jokes with the van driver through his open window, as though to endorse his slightly illegal yet eminently practical parking. Both of them ignore Terri and Richard, the white-collar office workers in their flashy car with a puncture.

Terri wishes she'd thought to park on the pavement, out of the way. By comparison, her parking spot on the curve of the mini-roundabout seems awkward and absurd. After a short time the policewoman drives away and the van driver reads his paper. Terri folds her arms. She and Richard stare at the rain covering the windscreen.

*

A tow truck turns up after forty minutes and stops close to the car. Terri immediately opens the door and gets out, glad to break the atmosphere that has developed with Richard.

The mechanic is almost bald but has a lot of hair. It trails from the bottom of his skull in long wispy sheaves. A tusk medallion is visible on his chest in the middle of his blue overalls. He scuttles up, spider-like, checks the damaged tyre, and peers into the car as though expecting to talk to the man. Richard continues to stare ahead, apparently happy to let Terri sort it out.

'Nasty smell!' The mechanic looks at the tyre and whistles. 'How long were you driving on him?' His voice is high-pitched.

The burnt rubber stinks of transgression.

'Don't know,' says Terri. 'A while.'

'You got the spare and the jack? And the alloy wheel nut sockets?'

He goes back to the boot without waiting for her to answer and soon emerges with what looks like a toy wheel, with yellow wording around its side.

'Temporary wheel. It'll do you but you need to stay under fifty and I wouldn't advise any sudden turns.' He lifts his face to the sky: the drizzle is continuing. 'Especially in the wet.' He bounces the temporary tyre on the ground and rests it against the car. 'I'll look in the glove compartment for those sockets.' He scurries away.

Terri gives Richard a dirty look through the side window, but he's still staring ahead.

From the other side of the car the mechanic whistles again. 'This one's got illegal tread. He's as bald as I am. When's the last time you had a service?'

He says this with relish as though it's a favourite taunt he makes to broken-down drivers, a perk of the job.

*

'When *did* you last take this in for a service?' she says, when the mechanic has gone, and they're both back in the car.

Richard holds out his hands. 'Do you really want me to answer that?'

'It is your car.'

'It's a pool car. Any of us can drive it.'

'It's your pool car. And none of this would've happened if we hadn't stopped for fuel. We'd have been in a different place when the ambulance passed. We wouldn't have picked up the nail.'

He's about to rage again but then he sets his jaw. 'I've had it,' he says, opening the car door.

'What are you doing?' The finality of his tone has spread into her own voice.

'What's it look like? Getting out. Going it alone. On foot.'

'We're in the middle of nowhere.'

He taps his mobile phone. 'This thing knows where I am.' He pinches the screen. 'Maidenhead railway station is two miles away. Over there.'

Glancing back, he says, 'It's for the best.'

Then he hops over a greasy crash barrier and strides off across the grass, glancing down at his phone as he goes. His gilet clings to his lean torso. Terri gets out to watch him go. She thuds her fist on top of the car.

*

From the service depot she goes all the way around the motorway junction and back along the dual carriageway. She leaves the stereo off. Since the car seems to have become her responsibility, she wants to find a garage to replace the temporary tyre. But most of all she wants to go home. She's lost all interest in the team meeting.

There is a slight instability in the car that she puts down to the thin temporary tyre on the driver's side. Or perhaps she's imagining it. Fifty miles per hour has never seemed so slow as she trundles along the inside lane, cars, vans, even articulated lorries piling up behind and then overtaking. She has no way to communicate to the other drivers why she is going so slowly, and it's as though their impatience and irritation is being transmitted into the car and into her head.

The rain settles into a fine drizzle. She finds herself allowing the speed to increase — first to sixty and then to seventy. It's a reasonable compromise between the eighty or ninety miles per hour she would usually do and the maximum safety speed printed on the sides of the tyre. No longer the slowest vehicle on the road, she moves into the fast lane to pass a dawdling Rover and ends up staying there.

Where is Richard now? She pictures him leaping over crash barriers in his gilet, or finding his mobile phone has led him to some impenetrable barrier of trunk roads.

The same intense sadness comes over her that she experienced earlier in the car. This time there is no reason to suppress it. She lets the tears run down her face and drives her foot into the accelerator pedal as she breaks into sobs. It feels therapeutic, a release, and she lets it all out.

Her thoughts are interrupted by a violent knocking sound from the outside of the car.

Thuc-thuc-thuc-thuc.

Suffering a pang of guilt about her speed on the temporary tyre, she swears and pulls from the fast lane to the inside and then onto the hard shoulder, the knocking sound continuing all the way. She waits for a break in the traffic and pushes the door open, slides out, slams it shut and runs around the car to the verge. A lorry storms past, rocking the parked car. She opens the passenger door and activates the hazard lights. During another traffic break she goes round to examine the thin temporary tyre with the yellow safety wording. It's still inflated and shows no sign of damage. She peers under the wheel arch in case a branch or other rubbish has got caught up and is causing the knocking sound. Nothing. The drizzle continues and the far side of the motorway is fuzzy with mist. Perhaps the act of pulling over has dislodged whatever obstruction was causing the noise. More in hope than expectation, she gets back in. She pulls away with the hazards on, straight along the hard shoulder.

Thuc ... Thuc ... Thuc-thuc-thuc.

The sound starts again, the intervals decreasing as she speeds up. She leans her head towards the steering wheel and realises that the sound is not coming from the temporary tyre but from the front passenger side. Sighing, she pulls over again, this time taking the car right onto the verge at the side of the tarmac.

She inspects the other wheel. There's no puncture but something is sticking up at the back of the tyre. She reaches in and pulls out a long thin strip of rubber, noticing as she does so the lack of tread on this tyre, just as the mechanic said earlier. The rubber strip is still attached to the tyre and she can't yank it off. She's not sure whether it's a significant problem or something that just happens, some skin shredding. But it is undoubtedly the cause of the knocking sound and she doesn't feel comfortable to continue without getting it checked out.

The rain soaks into her hair. She gets the heavy blue coat from the back seat and puts it on, once again glad of its warmth and protection. Without Richard to give her a second opinion she has no choice but to call the breakdown service. She dreads being put through to the same operator as before.

It's too noisy to make the call by the car, and besides she wants to get as far away from the traffic as possible. Next to the hard shoulder a bank slopes up, covered in bushes and small trees. She climbs it and reaches a wire fence which overlooks a flat field with half a dozen cows, an incongruous sight in the context of the motorway. Drops of rain build up on the branches of the trees at the top of the bank and land on her head. She tries to find the position with the fewest drips and pulls out her mobile phone. Soon she's listening to the same jazzy on-hold music that she heard just a couple of hours previously. It occurs to her that the same mechanic will be asked to scuttle out again. Oh well. This day is testing her philosophical nature. She forces herself to take a deep breath.

As the music continues, she gazes at her surroundings. The traffic blasts past, barely any quieter up here than by the car. Bleached-out fast food cartons are scattered on the ground. The bank is a hostile and polluted environment, not meant to be seen by humans. An extra-large raindrop falls down the back collar of her coat. She looks up at the tree and notices something strange about the trunk. It is completely coated with a thick green layer of lichen.

Last seen unpacking 'Uncle Dougie's Suitcase' in our anthology And Nothing Remains, *Alastair Chisholm is making not one but two welcome returns in this volume.*

The Castle

Alastair Chisholm

He marked out the curtain wall first, straight and square, scraping his stick carefully through thick, damp sand. Then the inner keep, and the entrance. Down at the water, Daisy splashed and kicked spray, but he ignored her. He studied the outline for a few seconds, frowning.

'Have you put on sun cream?' his mother asked. He grunted in reply, and started digging the outer ditch. Then stopped, as a shadow moved across him.

'Looking good,' said the man.

The boy glowered. The sand was tiny shells, pricking into his knees, salt on his cheeks. He finished the ditch and moved around to the front.

'Micky, play with me!' shouted Daisy. 'Play catch with me, Micky!'

'In a minute,' called the man. He looked down. 'What's this bit?'

'Barbican,' the boy muttered.

'Like, shops?' asked the man, frowning.

The boy snorted. 'No, stupid.'

'James!' His mother's voice, sharp and embarrassed. 'Don't be rude.'

He shrugged.

'It's a defensive tower,' she said. 'We looked it up in a book, didn't we, James? In Wales, last year. We stayed near a lovely beach, made castles all week.'

The barbican guarded the main entrance, with its own ditch and tall walls. He added crenellations, a finger-width apart, and arrow slits carved into the side. Behind him the man sat down again, next to his mother.

'I'm sorry,' she said, her voice lower. 'Maybe this wasn't a good idea. But Janet couldn't babysit, I thought —'

'Nah, it's good. Haven't been to the beach in years.'

'It's not very romantic, ha-hah!' She sounded nervous.

James finished the outer wall and began to dig inside.

'That's just how it is these days.' The man's voice was magnanimous, pleased to be doing a favour. 'Modern relationships, and that. Everyone's got baggage.'

James piled up sand to build the keep, within the castle. Twice as tall as the curtain walls, and stronger.

'You can make it up to me later, ay?' Male laughter, wet kissing noises, and her squirming giggle.

'Cheeky! Who says there's going to be a later?' But she didn't sound cross. The boy scowled and attacked the sand with his spade.

'Micky! Come and play, Micky!' called Daisy from the water.

'In a bit, darlin'!' Then, lower: 'I'm playing with your Mum just now.'

'Stop it!' More giggling. 'Micky, stop it, really, he's right *there —*'

'Ach! Yeah, all right.' A sigh, and a whip-spray of sand as the man kicked to his feet. 'Okay, Daisy, I'm comin'.'

The boy found two small curled shells, whorls of brown and white, and placed them on the wall of the keep, and next to them a piece of green beach glass, clouded and smoothed by the sea. He scooped sand to the corners and carved towers. His mother knelt beside him; she smelled of sun cream and freshly washed hair.

'Hey, Jamie,' she said, softly. 'Can I help?'

He shrugged. She reached across to the wall with one bare arm. Her skin was pale, with tiny smears of white cream; her shoulders narrow; the red and green stripe of her bikini strap bright against her neck. She was wearing perfume too, he realised. Too sweet: the scent of babysitters and new dresses and jewellery, and *be good, might be back late.*

'Micky! Mum, Micky's fallen over!' Daisy laughing, and the man laughing too.

'Help! Argh!'

His mother watched them and smiled. 'He's trying to be friendly,' she murmured. 'Daisy likes him.'

'You're breaking the wall,' he said. 'You're breaking the wall, stop it!'

'Oops, sorry, love. Here, I'll fix it ...'

'You're breaking the *wall!*' He gave her a huge shove, and she sprawled back onto the sand.

'For god's sake, James!'

'Everything okay?' The man again.

'Yes, yes.' She sounded cross. 'Just someone being a bit rude.'

'Oh. Um ... Hey, what about ice creams?'

'Yes! Ice creams, yes!' Daisy's voice, ecstatic. 'Can I have a ninety-nine?'

'Sure. What about you, James? Ice cream?'

He shook his head, but the man didn't give up. 'What's this part inside?' he asked, pointing.

The boy was silent.

'James, answer him,' said his mother. '*James*. Oh, you're being ridiculous. It's the keep — it's like a castle inside the castle.'

'Oh right, where the king lives, yeah?' The man crouched next to him: large feet, legs wet and covered in thick dark hair, crusted with sand; bare arms; bare chest; deodorant and sweat and drips of wet hair gel. Right next to him, almost touching. He moved away.

'No.'

'Micky!' shouted Daisy. 'Play catch, Micky!'

'No? Then who?'

'Micky!'

He didn't answer at first. Then he pointed to the shells, and the smooth green glass pebble. 'Prince and princess,' he muttered. 'Queen.' He glared up into the man's face. 'No king.'

The man looked back at him. He smiled again; but a different smile, now. Thoughtful.

'Is that right?'

'Micky, catch!'

And a quick hard shadow, a ball —

'Ah, shit!' The man swung back on his haunches, lost his balance. White arms swinging, reaching out, then over-balancing, and he toppled ...

He tried to catch himself with one hand, all his weight going into the side of the keep; his knee crashed through the curtain wall and flattened it.

'Shit! Sorry!' Laughing. 'God, sorry, ha-hah!'

The boy gasped in horror.

'Daisy, look what you did!' His mother, cross and anxious.

'It wasn't me! It was Micky!'

'Yeah, my fault,' the man said. 'Sorry!'

'Jamie? Jamie, love?'

He stared at the wreckage. The walls were breached, the ditch filled, the keep shattered; one shell buried under the sand, lost, the other lying next to the glass pebble.

'It's okay, love. We can mend it.'

Daisy said, 'We can make a new castle, can't we, Micky? We can make one together.'

'Course, darlin'.' He looked at the boy and shrugged. 'Sorry, mate. Hey — let's rescue the queen, eh?' And he reached across and plucked her away, leaving the shell behind.

'Come on,' he said, standing. 'Ice creams.'

*In his first story for The Fiction Desk. Matt Harris
reminds us that the threads we follow as we make our
way through life can also be used to follow us.*

Broken Pixel

Matt Harris

I am looking for a silence. I've sensed it a dozen times in passing, but a silence is a hard thing to pin down. This silence is not in the physical world, but in the world of data, the world of electronic communication. That's where I spend my time.

Data can be a dry and difficult thing to work with, even for someone like me. That's why we create visualisations of it. We have a system that can visualise everything: all of the electronic information being exchanged all over our planet, rushing through cables, piling up in servers, filling the air. Immense quantities of data, zettabytes and yottabytes of it, more and more with every passing moment.

You can choose how the visualisation appears, but since I have an artistic kind of temperament I see it as a colourful three-dimensional world through which I can move at will. I call it the data world. There are purple mountains of stored information, yellow rivers of communications data, nodes that resemble huge metal spiderwebs, literal firewalls burning fifty feet high. This is where I work.

The data world is noisy, because it's populated. We call them profiles, and they look just like people. Each one is composed of the data broadcast by, received by, and referencing a single human being. Everybody has one now. Most are very noisy: constantly shouting out their every thought and feeling, sharing their purchases, their movements, their entertainment preferences, documenting and broadcasting their every living moment with as much detail and as much volume as they can muster.

It's against this cacophony that I've sensed that silence. It's more a vague feeling than anything ... a realisation: *someone I just passed was different.* Yet each time I got that feeling, I turned and saw only the clamorous crowd.

*

I am a spy, a good one. It's what I was made to do. At the moment, in a manner of speaking at least, I am working for the British state. It's more accurate to say that I work for Tenniel North, a data mining company owned by Waghdas Systems, a very large corporation itself a part of Levelin, one of the three largest tech companies in the world. Tenniel North is currently contracted by the British state for espionage purposes. Most governments outsource that kind of thing these days. They outsource nearly everything, in fact. The state is withering away, though not quite in the manner that Engels imagined.

So the work I do is notionally for Britain. It seems archaic to be working for a nation, but it's a good business move. They pay us, of course, but for Tenniel North and Levelin, the fee isn't the valuable thing. What's valuable is the data we collect.

Some of my colleagues are abroad, stealing secrets from other nations to pass to the British. Some of them are here, engaged in counter-espionage, battling foreign spies who are trying to steal secrets from Britain. I am spying on our own citizens: the fastest-growing sector in the espionage industry.

*

I am moving through the data world: following leads, meeting moles, speaking with contacts, looking for threats.

The data world is dynamic, ever-moving. Buildings adjust themselves as you pass, reconfiguring like puzzle boxes. Hills swell, valleys veer, forests crawl up mountainsides or sink and liquefy, becoming lakes. Roads constantly branch, or sometimes change direction as you follow them. Concrete flyovers spring out from hills to arc over villages. The landscape shifts and rolls in response to big news stories, stock market action, system updates. And the colours — they never stop moving. The hills might be green one moment and yellow the next. Blue roads blush red as their traffic increases. The sky swirls with ribbons of colour like oil on water. Sometimes you can tell what's going on from the colours; you can feel the mood of the information world.

Against this gaudy landscape the profiles frolic and fight. They stand on hills and shout, they lie down and sleep, they form mobs, they project images of their real-world activity. Most of all they talk. They don't listen much, except to celebrity profiles, and sometimes to an unfortunate that calls out something the crowd doesn't like. Within moments a mob of millions can form around a single profile and tear it apart in a violent frenzy. Lynchings happen almost daily.

The average terrorist or radical broadcasts their beliefs to the open web for ten hours a day, so tracking them down is not difficult. The greater part of my job for the British is done for me by my suspects. Their profiles stand on hills in the data world shouting slogans, waving flags. I watch them, follow them, file reports.

There are cannier radicals of course, those who communicate through darknets. In the data world, these encrypted networks appear as basements, sewer systems, bunkers, and caves. I am heading towards one now.

Becoming invisible, I approach a cliff that overlooks a flickering sea. I follow a rocky path down into a cave on the cliff face, where a dozen profiles are meeting. This cave represents a highly encrypted network used by a number of Islamist extremist groups. I can enter it with ease because it was actually built by Levelin. Extremists of all kinds are a valuable market and keen early adopters of social technology, so the company is keen to cater to them. An exact copy of this network exists nearby, appearing as another cave: that one is used by Christian extremist groups. I imagine some software engineer at Levelin was amusing himself when he created this set-up.

The profiles in the cave today are all braggarts and fakers. They are discussing terrorist attacks that none of them know how to carry out. I log and record the activity and move on.

I visit a pale, papery forest on a quiet plain. This is where a group of environmental activists regularly meet. I find them seated in a circle discussing their imminent prosecution for trespass. Despite their advocacy of the simple life, all these profiles are extremely bright, indicating the humans behind them spend a great deal of time broadcasting themselves online. Each profile wears a balaclava, representing use of client-side encryption that makes them anonymous. The balaclavas are made by a Chinese subsidiary of Levelin and naturally the firm passed the required encryption key to my department. The key appears in my hand now; it is knitted from the same black wool as the balaclavas. The data world is not without a sense of whimsy.

I sit with the activists invisibly. Squeezing the woollen key causes the balaclavas to become transparent to me. I identify each profile, then search through the information I have on them, which is comprehensive and mostly volunteered by the subjects themselves. In particular, their purchase histories have Levelin written all over them.

I sit for a while as they chat about the court case. They reveal some illegal practices of the energy company that's prosecuting them. I send this information to my superiors, with a recommendation that copies be forwarded to Levelin's energy subsidiaries for leverage purposes.

The British see these environmentalists as dangerous radicals. As with the Islamists, Levelin's view is subtly different. Malcontents they may be, but both groups are keen and sophisticated users of our products. We watch them for our British client, but we never forget their status as valued customers.

*

I move on, towards a valley full of moving architecture that's especially dense with profiles. An information city. This is the area where I first sensed that silence.

There are a couple of reasons that a person's profile might be quiet in the data world. They might be extremely old. Plenty of old people live their lives online now, where their decrepitude matters less, but a small number are entirely offline – mostly the truly ancient, the last people to grow up without the internet, ninety-year-olds nearing their end in care homes. They have profiles composed of their banking information, medical records ... but they are faint, almost transparent things, and they get rarer by the day.

A quiet profile might also belong to a hermit of some kind. Most reclusive humans are very active in the data world, but some pursue a life in the wilderness, existing in some wretched hut without a single screen, no way of receiving data except looking out of the window. Usually it's just a phase. They come back to civilisation eventually, and in the data world their profiles come to life.

Or the quiet profile could belong to someone who's mentally incapable, comatose, kidnapped, imprisoned in some repressive state, or dead but not yet discovered. These unlikely cases aside, one possibility remains: someone is up to no good. That's why I'm paid to follow the silence.

The state's attitude to a quiet profile is one of deep suspicion. We have an infrastructure that allows all of us to broadcast ourselves to the world constantly, at every moment of the day, even while sleeping, and almost everybody has opted in to it. So as far as the state is concerned, anyone who opts out has something to hide, and is probably a threat. If they had their way, they would make silence a crime in itself. I'm reminded of Meursault, condemned because he didn't cry at his mother's funeral. *But he was a killer after all,* our British clients would say. *No smoke without fire!*

It's a coarse approach, but perhaps it's a necessary one. There are not many ways to draw suspicion upon yourself any more. You can do almost anything you like, be any kind of person you want, as long as you don't do it unwatched. Everything is permitted, nothing is private.

That's the way the state looks at it, anyway. Me? I'm not the judgemental type. I just like information.

*

Today, as I move through the chaotic streets of the information city, I am lucky. Amidst the noise I sense that peculiar lull, that silence, and this time I find the source: there it is, the profile in question, sitting on a shimmering crystal seat alongside the main thoroughfare. There are countless seats the same, each representing a kind of rest-stop for a profile that is not currently active.

This profile is pale, almost transparent, and featureless. You could just about describe it as female. Using the technology at my disposal, I interrogate the profile without it becoming aware of my presence. It belongs to a human being named Carmella Morel. I search our records quickly, while I stand observing the profile from a safe distance. All around me a cacophony rages: people telling each other how tired they are, how offended they are, how much they hate a celebrity or how much they love their holidays or families or phones, while Carmella sits there like some bipedal jellyfish, quietly alive. For some reason the sky darkens to a rich purple as I stand watching her, and in response the buildings around me glow yellow.

My search results are in. Carmella's age, address, employer, and financial situation are now known to me, and are ordinary. She has never been arrested or suspected of a crime, is not known to associate with anyone who has. I search through her beliefs, alignments, relationships, feelings ... and get nothing. Nothing! Extraordinary.

Carmella hasn't done a thing in the data world beyond what the law requires. She hasn't broadcast a single thing about herself. She is quite transparent to me.

*

A short conference with my superior takes place, and it is recommended that I investigate Carmella. But to investigate someone who is barely present in the data world is difficult. This is one of those rare occasions when a human being might be more useful than me. Indeed, we do have some human agents at Tenniel North, whose shortcomings are offset by their possession of actual physical bodies that can walk down streets. But I'm not ready to call for help from a mammal just yet. I have methods for looking at the physical world too.

Carmella lives in North London. Flicking through satellite images and street photos, I move down into the area where she lives, then hook into a live feed of her street from a CCTV camera outside a corner shop. This camera provides a high-definition colour picture, unlike the relics elsewhere in the city. The corner shop must be making good money. I make a mental note to examine their financial activity for any hints of laundering.

After the data world, reality is so very flat and colourless. A dreary grey street, a few people walking up and down looking at their phones. There is Carmella's house. I sniff. Her house has an ordinary data connection. I detect a television in there. I activate its simple camera and connect live to its feed. The picture is extremely low resolution, but there is her living room, perfectly normal, and I can see a stereo and a laptop. She's not a primitivist or hermit then. The house is silent: she's obviously not in.

I move into her neighbour's house. It's full to the brim with active, much-used technology, so I can construct a nice high-definition feed of every room. I listen to them talking, watch them cook, watch them eat in front of their screens. I visit their profiles in the data world, examine their activity records over the past six months — every message, email, status, phone call — looking for references to Carmella. I do the same for every household in the street. I don't get much.

Anthony Rawlison complained in June that Carmella rarely moves her bin back into her yard after bin day. Noella Khader across the street muttered several times while alone in her front room that Carmella hadn't left her enough space after parking her car. A few other neighbours mentioned her in passing (*Just saw Carmella, she says hi ... Carmella said her holiday was nice*) and Barbara Johnson in the house opposite made several dozen racist posts on social media about Carmella, whom she mistakenly believes is Hispanic (*spic bitch parkin her bran new car across my drive agen probly got it free handout smh #opendoor #overrun*).

I learn next to nothing about Carmella. For a while I watch her house from outside, hoping she might return. It's Saturday so she's probably not at work (she's a finance assistant for a vocational college).

I return to the data world to find some of Carmella's friends. This is not difficult. Each profile is linked to thousands of others by glowing threads, which represent online interaction. The threads are bright but weightless; you can walk right through them. They are of infinitely variable length, and their thickness indicates the strength of the relationship: a rope for a close friend, a wispy line for someone you once emailed about a job. Carmella's profile, of course, has no threads at all, but her neighbours have plenty.

From her neighbours I scan out at high speed through networks of acquaintances and friends, trawling through records of what each has said online, looking for Carmella's name. It takes less than a minute to identify six profiles who are likely to be close friends of hers. One, Christine Parson, is sitting on a crystal seat, inactive, which suggests she's talking to someone in the physical world. Her last action was to share a photograph of a cappuccino with the words 'catch up!' attached to it. With GPS I locate her phone in a coffee shop in London.

Activating her phone camera and microphone I see her sipping her coffee, and hear a voice that might be Carmella's, based on an estimate of its age and social class. Causing the phone to emit a rapid series of ultrasonic tones I create a rudimentary sonar system and construct a three-dimensional visualisation of the space, a little wavy and colourless but serviceable enough. I orient the visualisation so it seems I am floating in the centre of the cafe, and turn to look at the woman who is speaking.

Carmella, in the almost-flesh, looks like her passport photograph. She's talking about a play she has seen. I watch her as she talks, my quarry before me at last. She doesn't look unusual.

She and her friend talk for an hour, saying nothing out of the ordinary, then they leave the shop together. After a kiss, they part. Since Carmella has no connected device in her possession, I have no way of directly tracking her. Through nearby surveillance cameras and the phones of passers-by, I follow her as she walks through town. It's very tricky, but I manage it for about ten minutes until I lose her in a busy intersection.

The frustration is unusual. Losing anyone is rare enough, but Carmella isn't even trying to get lost, as far as I can tell. I return to the data world and approach her profile again, hoping it might say something that leads me to Carmella. If she would just mention the park she's in, or check in at a bar, or even share a purchase she makes in a shop, as so many others do all day long. Nothing.

*

I report Carmella to the British intelligence services. I tell them of her suspicious silence. They are interested, of course, but someone like her can only be watched in the real world, and that is an expense the state struggles to afford. Her name is added to a long list of low-level persons of interest.

I keep an eye on her myself, as best I can. In the data world her profile remains silent. Through the many devices carried by her friends and colleagues I watch her, listen to her, and try to build a picture of her motivations. After six months of surveillance I come to the conclusion that she is neither a spy nor a terrorist, neither Luddite, radical, nor recluse. She lives a normal life, and makes a reasonable use of technology, but she has an abnormal lack of interest in sharing herself with others.

Her eccentricity on the matter is well known to her friends and colleagues, who occasionally question her or tease her on it. She has a rote answer that gives nothing away (*Oh I don't bother with all that*) but she won't be moved. In an odd way I admire her intransigence. As the months pass I almost feel that I know her. How absurd for me to know someone who barely even exists in the information world! But how intriguing, too.

Yet as much as her uniqueness appeals to me, I can't let it be. With just a little twinge of sadness, I pass her details on to a group of specialist colleagues. Their job is to make her a bit more like everyone else.

It's really nothing sinister: they will just manoeuvre her towards sharing more information. Carmella herself will never even know it's happening. She will simply encounter difficulties because of her silence in the data world: applications turned down, questions asked at work, purchases declined. Her primitive phone will keep malfunctioning, her television too. Just tiny frustrations, but ones that will disappear as soon as she upgrades, creates accounts, joins in, starts sharing. The whole process is very light-touch. It's something we excel at. We have, after all, been doing it to whole nations for half a century. Now we just focus on those left over, the stubborn individuals like Carmella.

You might ask why. It's a question I used to ask myself, but I think I have the answer now. There is an old saying that power corrupts — but it's truer to say power *purifies*. A powerless person might have a head full of desires and ideals and fears, but the more power they accrue, the more those things fall away. Eventually they desire only more power, and fear only the loss of power. Power seeks power, it purifies those who have it. With their ideals abandoned, the powerful will commit any outrage in exchange for more power, as history tells.

Knowledge is a form of power, but a benign one. A lust for data can't harm anyone, but otherwise the mechanism is similar. You start off gathering knowledge for a purpose — to improve yourself, to make money for your company — but eventually all you want is more knowledge. The means becomes the end. We make money from our data, it's true, but that hardly matters any more. What we desire is simply more and more data. Every little gap in our information picture is painful to us. Imagine a screen, infinitely broad: filling the sky forever in every direction, blazing white with pure information. Every Carmella is a broken pixel on that screen, a little black spot. Infuriating to look at.

Carmella will be worked on until finally she begins to engage like everybody else. She'll find life easier as she begins to use our products to broadcast herself to the world, and since we carefully engineer them to reward compulsion, she will use them more and more. She'll tell us all about herself: where she is, what she wants, how she thinks. Yes, we are meddlesome, but she won't be harmed — all we want is to understand her, to know her. Eventually we will know everyone. We will know everything.

*Our Newcomer Prize writing competition had its final outing
last year, making Lahra Crowe's story about the interaction
between language and thought our final winner. Between this and
Poppy Toland's story, the competition has gone out in style.*

Seelence

Lahra Crowe

It's a wee bit place, this hoose, up the braes that ur aye purple wi
heather an oan the lip ay the warld wi the salty, cauld grey water
slappin an roarin oantae the shore, an the stievie seaweed an the
shells an the torched rocks swirlin an tangled aroon the sand, as
though it's a mosaic, an the warld a muckle great art piece, baith
crafted by God's ain haun. It's a wee bit place, richt enough, whur
the cloods ur moody an the sky looks bruised maist ay the time, in
whorls ay purples, blues an greys, an the gulls skirl in the sky, an
the sun, when ye can see it, dreeks the hale landscape in glowin
pinks, oranges an reds, glowerin at ye afore dreepin seelently doon
beyond the dark easin. It's ma wee bit place.

It's the seelence ah love. The stillness. The total aloneness
wi nature. Iain an me, we'd aye sit fur oors up the brae, cooried
thegither wi jackets, scarves, gloves an hats keepin us warm, an jist
stare forever at the dayset, an listen tae the cauld rush ay wind,

73

feelin it nippin oor coupons, an love the fresh sting ay the sea kelp, at yin wi nature, an at yin wi each other. We'd breathe it aw in wioot speakin, an awhiles draw or paint, awhiles write, awhiles read, but aye be content.

Folk said when we moved here fae the city that we'd git bored, that it'd be tae dreich, that we'd need company, that nature wouldnae be eneuch; that each other wouldnae be eneuch. They whur wrang. Fur near oan eighteen year we stayed here an whur niver bored, niver needed onythin else. It wis braw tae see friends, braw tae see family, braw tae go intae the toon bytimes at the weekends, but it wis guid when they left tae, an we whur thegither jist the twa ay us at hame: Iain an me.

*

Ah'm thinkin oan aw ay this when Ah go fur a wee daunder this mornin doon by the rocks. It's jist warm enough fur me tae dip ma feet intae the water. Ah love how the slicin cauld soothes yer skin, an Ah love watchin the birsie white froth papple and sotter as it crashes and foams aroon yer feet, an Ah love the snell salty air, an the haar that creeps o'er bytimes in the morning, an Ah love the soond ay the waves skelpin the shore. Maistly but, it's the sittin still, awhiles fur oors, oan the black rocks that Ah'm in love wi — no havin tae move until Ah feel like movin, jist drinkin it aw up, jist enjoyin the warld. Iain understood that. He wis the same.

But the day Ah'm gettin ready tae go oot awa fur the weekend, so's Ah know Ah cannae sit fur lang, awtho Ah want tae. Forbye that, Ah dae jist potter aroon the hoose, takin a lang, hot bath an readin ma book, makin thoosands ay cups ay tea, scribblin doon some ideas fur a wee story ontae ma notepad, or paintin the odd wee stroke ontae ma picture. Ma easel's by the windae an it's slow work, cause wi the picture Ah'm daein the now Ah have tae wait fur the sun tae come oot – it disnae happen aw that often an, when it does, Ah only catch a few glisks, only get a few wee gowd brushtrokes in, afore the sun, that shy child, slinks gently ahint a clood again.

As Ah'm leavin the hoose, Ah catch sight ay the auld photo ay me an Iain sittin oan the mantle, an Ah pick it up. We're younger, alane, hair whipped back wi the wind, grinnin at the lens. God, Ah miss him. It's no that Ah feel alane maist ay the time, in the sense that ither people'd think ay it. Ah mean, Ah dae feel alane, but Ah like it. Ah ayewis have. It's no the company that Ah miss, it's *him*. Ah miss Iain. And, Ah think, the days when Ah miss him maist ur days like the day, when Ah have tae mingle wi people wha dinnae understaun it, wha make me feel alane in a different way awthegither.

*

Ah'm thinkin ay this as the landscape changes fae coast tae loch, as Ah drive the car doon oot ay the mist an see the hooses, peppered in the russet rid glens an the purple hills an the scabbit moors then, efter, clutterin the flattenin lands or spillin oot o'er the earth in a guddle ay bricks an concrete. The cloods drift awa an awtho the air's warmer, Ah feel caulder awready, stiffer, stentit. The rackit ay the engines an the breinge ay the lichts, the fowk, the fustiness ay the exhausts, it aw groans in oan me an Ah steady masel. It wis easier wi Iain, cos Ah knew he felt the same way, an when we left an drove hame we'd no spak a word the hale journey, an that wis okay.

As Ah drive up tae the hoose an get oot the car there's a shout fae the front door an a wee body comes chargin taewart me, screamin, 'Auntie Fi, Auntie Fi', an Ah pick it up an birl it roond an it giggles an shrieks. Ah dae it again, like it asks, an then move over tae gie ma sister, Louise, a hug, ignorin the same wee body atween us that's tuggin at ma jeans. Louise hauds me ticht an a feel a great warmth taewart her.

'It's guid tae see ye,' Ah say, genuinely.

'Yes, it is,' she says, wi a smile.

'Happy fortythird,' Ah say, handin over her present, 'auld timer'.

'Oooft,' she says, 'don't go down that road. Remember that you're not too far behind me. Before long we'll be as old as Mum.' She drops her voice at the last bit, as Mum shuffles oot ay the hoose tae greet me. 'Come on in. Everybody's out in the back garden.'

Ah go through tae the back garden, which is neat an trimmed wi a white fence tae gie us some privacy fae the hooses next door, and dozens of voices clamour over me fae across the lawn ... *Did you see the match on Saturday, Jamie? It was a ...* The lawn's mown tight an short an garden gnomes wave motionlessly from the tidy rock garden in the corner ... *Are you serious?! She's one to watch, just make sure* ... People sit in wee squares oan white, plastic chairs, delicately holdin cups an salads an glasses ay wine, an a million little things scrabble oan the ground playin an tumbling an screamin ... *I honestly can't remember the last time I had a proper sleep, or any time to myself* ... A mother shoogles a toddler, who screams and screams and screams ... *What is that one from the X Factor called, what's ...* and screams and screams ... *no, it was his first steps. David missed it, such a shame.* Ah move around the garden, away from them all ... *The M25's a nightmare though, Joanne, no wonder* ... Ah sip ma wine slowly, watchin everybody, zonin out of the conversation goin on beside me, the one Ah'm supposedly involved in ... *I just know it. I don't care what ...* The children are exhausting, even from here ... *Lucy goes through so many nappies, I'm telling you, she's ...* The older ones run around like mad people, screaming and shouting and a younger one, a baby, plays more quietly on the mat. It stops and stares at me, as impassively as Ah'm watching it, its bald, alien head movin unsteadily from side tae side ... *Derek's getting all As in his schoolwork at the moment, yes, he wants to be an engineer ...* A bit ay drool falls from its bottom lip. I feel really quite repulsed.

'You know, it's not too late.'

'What?' I say, as Ah turn round and see Louise perched beside me on the wall. I know what's coming though.

'It's not too late,' she repeats. 'To have one. A baby.'

I pause and consider her. I consider my response. She's looking at me pityingly and Ah can see that she means well. She's probably been planning this conversation for weeks.

'Louise, Ah ...'

'Look, I know what you're going to say, but you don't need a man these days. They've got these things called sperm banks, where you can just go and ...' I stare at her, irritated that she thinks I don't know what a sperm bank is, and angry that nobody, not even my own sister, understands. I think of all the books that I've read, and the places that I've travelled to (both with Iain and on my own), everything I've learned being so close to nature, of all the worldly knowledge I have that my 'big' sister – who lives in a box and spends her days speaking the way she has been told to, living the life she is expected to, surrounded by meaningless noise, changing nappies, reading *Heat* magazine and watching *X Factor* on the TV – does not realise I have. As I stare at her, it is a minute or two before I notice my mother has also come over, and is watching me intently. '... you'd have me,' Louise continues, 'and John too, and if you moved down here again then ...'

'Louise,' I interrupt, 'I don't want a wean'. There is a moment or two where she and my mother exchange a look with each other, a look that plainly tells me it is not just Louise who has been planning this conversation. In the pause, the chatter from across the garden drifts over to us *... I've applied for a promotion, think I've got a good chance ...* Louise leans forward.

'Fi, you don't understand yet, that it's the most wonderful thing in the world. Being a mother, it ... it changes everything. You might not think you want one now, but when you hold your little one in your arms for the first time, it just ... completes you.' She's gazing at me earnestly and I know that nothing I can ever say will persuade her that, for me, that just wouldn't be true.

'When we were wee,' I say carefully, 'you aye really wanted weans. Do you mind playin wi oor dolls in the back garden? Do you mind when Auntie Jeanie had wee Gareth? Mind how much you wanted tae hold him, and change his nappy and play wi him?' She nods. 'But *I* didn't, Louise, an I still don't.' She opens her mouth to argue with me, but I press on. 'Mind that time as well, years ago, when we had been out dancing and you'd had too much to drink? You were greetin cos ye said your life was just empty, and you didnae know what the point of ...'

'Fiona,' my mother interrupts, '*please* speak properly. You need to stop this! Iain's been gone for two years now. You need to move on with your life, while you still can,' she adds, sharply. Because, of course, I think angrily, having a baby is the only thing my life can move on to, and I will never be able to 'move on' with my life when I am too old to have children.

'Mum, I, Ah didn't want weans when Iain wis here, an Ah still don't now an —'

'Have you ever thought that maybe Iain would still be alive now if he'd had more to live for?' My mother cuts in, in that curt, cold, clipped way that only she can, and for a second I can feel my breath freeze painfully in my lungs. 'What do you really have up there, on your own?'

'I cannae believe you just said that.' I stand up dizzily, feeling sick with rage and, like always, sucked into it all, feeling the pressure close in around me, choking me, crushing me. I stare at them, predatory spiders weaving sticky threads, thirsting to bleed. 'I'm leavin.' I pull on my coat and begin to pick my way across the grass, through the ordered maze of plastic cups, plates, toys and children, ignoring Louise's and my mother's calls behind me. I'm coldly aware of everybody staring at me, of dozens of sets of eyes watching me, Louise's oddball sister, callously storm out on her birthday. I can feel the criticism in their glares: I don't know what I'm missing; I'm going to regret this later; I'm selfish; I'll die alone and miserable. Well, perhaps I might die miserable, but so might they. So might anyone.

I get into my car and slam the door on Louise's tears. I just want to get out of here. I savour the silence in the car and I breathe a couple of huge sighs as I leave the city. All around me grey tower blocks loom ominously, silhouetted against an even darker, greyer sky. The grey concrete road stretches out rigidly in front of me. Grey pylons with grey wires crisscross overhead and grey cars carrying empty grey people slip past me on the road. Ah look longingly at the warmin purplish peaks in the distance. Ah relish the richness ay the silence in the car an at the same time, Ah grieve fur Iain's seelence, which isnae here, which would've made it full. Weans, screamin, whinin weans, or even laughin, singin weans, would drain the car, drain the seelence, no fill it. Even bairns that whur ma ain would dae that. Even bairns that whur mine's an Iain's. The only yin, the only person in the warld wha can fill that seelence is Iain, an he's no here now save an ill dwaum in ma throat an a stoondin, loupin, achin somewhere sae deep in ma body that Ah cannae place it. God, an Ah miss him sae much, an Ah jist miss him sae, sae much.

But as Ah get tae Crianlarich, an the moon, the glowin, silvery moon, rests gently oan tap ay the mountain peaks, Ah feel calm. Ah think aboot how tae express the truths that Ah know: that life is gorgeous an precious an slips awa fae us like water through oor fingers; that life is sae much mair than jist people; that we only have wan short wee breath afore we wither an crumble back intae the stoory dust we came fae. That, cause ay that, havin a wean jist isnae richt fur me. Ah know it, an Iain knew it wisnae fur us either, when he wis alive. An, aye, Ah miss him. Aye, Ah grieve fur him sae much ma hairt cannae haud it aw bytimes, but that's jist life. A wean that Ah jist dinnae want willnae change that. It wouldnae bring back Iain, an Iain's the only thing Ah want, the only thing Ah've ever wanted, the only thing Ah will ever want.

Ah turn the car aff the road near tae ma hoose an stap. Pullin ma hikin boots oan, Ah tramp up the brae a wee bit an roond the side until Ah get a fine view ay the coast. The water's shiverin fae the wind's cauld touch an the moonlicht quivers oan the surface, blanchin wee strips so's it looks like threads ay the finest eevory silk ur lipperin and pirlin oan the tap ay it. As Ah sit still a dark wee pine martin daunders awa hyne, an a hoolet screeches somewhere tae the left. The heather's crisp an springy under ma hauns, an, as ever, the air's aw fresh an salty an free an Ah know that, if Ah live that lang, Ah'll be here anither eighteen year, only this time oan ma ain. An that's no sae bad. Ah tak oot ma sketchbook an charcoal an smudge a few wee lines ontae the page, tryin, as ayewis, tae capture the beauty an stillness an wildness an magic ay the warld, ay Scotland. An the seelence fills ma hale body like honey.

Sometimes we rely so heavily on the thread we're following that we become entangled and can't let go even when something is clearly wrong, as in the second part of our Alastair Chisholm double bill.

Exhalation

Alastair Chisholm

Tuesday.

There's condensation all the way up the windows: a thick, greasy-white web that obscures the view and presses against the passengers. The bus is full, and I'm perched on the edge of a seat next to a fat man who sits with his legs apart, taking up most of the space. He stares at the window, though he can't see out. He's doing it so he doesn't accidentally make eye contact with me.

I hate the bus home. Everyone's tired and miserable, too drained even to be pleased about finishing work. They sit with their mouths open and their faces collapsed, steam rising off them, water trickling down their necks. Their clothes are crumpled and so is their hair, and their tempers, and their hope. And the journey stretches on forever, inching through endless traffic jams. I'm sure I could walk it quicker – I tell myself that one day I will – but commuter apathy grips me like the others.

Still, we're nearly at my stop. I stand and ring the bell, feeling the seat shift behind me as the man spreads his legs wider, claiming his territory. The bus shudders to a halt.

It's still raining, and I pull up my collar and trudge home, leaning against the wind. We should try to get a holiday before the baby comes. We've a while yet, it's only October. Somewhere warm; Portugal or something. That would be nice.

Thinking about holidays cheers me up and by the time I get home I've shaken off some of the lethargy. The door scrapes against post and newspapers as I open it: Jenny hasn't been out today. It's all junk and I bin it before heading in.

'Jenny? I'm home.'

'Hi Nick,' she calls from the sitting room. She's on the sofa, peering at an old knitting pattern and holding a skein of yellow wool and two needles rather uncertainly. When I come in she looks up at me and smiles, and the cold and weariness burn away in a moment. She's still in her dressing gown. She's gorgeous.

'Oi, woman!' I bellow. 'Where's my dinner?'

Jenny sticks her tongue out. 'I'm your wife, not your skivvy,' she says. 'Anyway, I'm doing motherly things. Knitting, see?' She waves the needles.

'Great!' I say. She's been trying for ages, without much success. 'Socks or scarf?'

She frowns. 'Maybe one big trouser leg,' she says, and I laugh. 'How's the bump?'

Jenny grins. 'She kicked again, after lunch.'

'Fantastic! Let's have a listen.'

I walk over but find I've stood on a little pile of flower petals; ground them into the carpet, almost.

'Oh god, sorry Nick,' says Jenny, 'I should have hoovered.'

'It's okay,' I say, and kiss her. 'I'll do it. You stay there, save your strength. Practice your knitting.'

I rummage through the closet. 'Where's the hoover?' I call.

'I think I had it in the study,' she says.

'Um, right,' I say. The study. I gaze at the coats and scarves for a second, then walk over to the study door and reach for the handle. I don't quite touch it.

It's stupid, really. Just ... recently, there's something about the study I don't like. I don't know why, but ... it's so *cold*. I haven't mentioned it, but I think Jenny knows. It's nothing I can put my finger on. Always so cold. Like, a feeling that if I enter I won't even be able to take a breath. Stupid.

I go back to the closet and pull out the dustpan and brush. When I return to the sitting room Jenny looks at me sympathetically.

'It's all right,' she says. 'I can get the hoover, if you like.'

'No, no, this is fine,' I say. I can't look her in the eye. 'I'll use this. It's fine.' I sweep up petals and tip them away.

'My poor hard-working Nicky,' she says. 'Come here.' I sit down beside her.

'Listen for the baby,' she says, and I rest my head on her smooth stretched belly and listen. I can't hear anything, but it's nice just to lie there. After a while I doze off, and when I wake up Jenny has gone to make the tea. The dustpan and brush are on the floor next to the sofa. I put them away and try not to look at the study door.

*

Wednesday.

My job is deathly boring. I sit all day in front of a computer, taking instructions from emails and turning them into instructions in other emails. I dimly recall a time when this seemed reasonable, even interesting, but I can't remember why. Now it's just something to do until I can go home again. I pick up a document and see that there's a stain on the cuff of my suit jacket. When did that happen?

I forgot to collect my clean suit from the dry-cleaner's yesterday evening. It's my fault: Jenny used to do it, but now she finds it harder to leave the house. So I have to do it, and I keep forgetting. It's this job, it dulls my head. The others here are the same. When I say hello, they look at me as if they can't understand how anyone could be happy here. Maybe they're overworked, or worried about staff cuts. Or perhaps it's the cold winter dark seeping in. Sometimes I try to lighten the mood, but I'm not much of a joke-teller and it always ends awkwardly.

I stick to data entry. It seems to go on forever, but oddly enough five o'clock comes around quite quickly. Another day gone, without even thinking about it. I head off, waving to the others. One or two of them watch me leave.

I remember to stop off at the dry-cleaner's, but when I get there I can't find my ticket. I walk back to the flat in the rain, trying to think what I could have done with it. When I get back there are more petals inside the door, swept in by the wind. I scoop them up and dump them outside. There's more post too, all bills. I come into the sitting room and wave them at Jenny.

'Reminders,' I say in mock admonishment. 'Your job. Have you been forgetting to pay the bills?'

Jenny grins. 'Too busy thinking about the baby,' she says. 'Shrinking brain.' She gives me a kiss. 'How was your day?'

I pour myself a whisky. 'The same,' I say.

'Aw, my poor love.'

I have to clear some stuff off the table to put my drink down: dirty glasses and takeaway boxes, and plates coated with food. The TV's on.

'Hey, do you know what happened to my dry-cleaning chitty?' I ask.

'Did you hand in your suit?'

'Yeah, of course. I mean ... I think so. Hang on.' I check upstairs, and am embarrassed to find it in the bedroom, in a crumpled dirty heap at the side of the bed. 'Huh. Guess not.'

'I'm not the only one with the shrinking brain, eh?' she calls up.

I stare at the suit. 'Yeah,' I say. I could have sworn I'd handed it in. It's a mess. I'll have to wear this one again.

I come back downstairs. 'You've changed your hair,' I say. She's pinned it up, like when we first met.

'I got bored with it down. Here, listen, she was kicking again.'

I come over to the sofa and rest my ear against her belly, but I can't hear anything. 'It could be a boy,' I say.

'No, it's a girl,' she says, with certainty. 'Definitely a girl.'

'Whatever you say,' I murmur.

From where I'm lying I realise I can see through the sitting room door and across the hall to the study, and for a moment I feel an odd queasy sensation; a tightness in my chest as if I've forgotten how to breathe. The door is closed, but I have the strangest image: that inside the study, someone is holding the handle, waiting; and if I looked away, the handle would turn ...

But Jenny rests her hand over my eyes until I close them, and the study goes away.

'Shh, my darling,' she whispers, stroking my head. 'Relax, love, you're home. Everything's all right.'

*

Tuesday.

No, wait. Thursday. What day is it? That's the problem with office life: time slips past you. Is it even October still? I've been feeling oddly run down lately. It's starting to show at work. I can't help it, it's so tedious; all I want to do when I'm here is get back to Jenny, back to our little flat.

The day drags along. In the afternoon Mr Matthews calls me into his office.

'How are you, Nick?' he asks.

I shrug. 'Fine. Busy, you know.'

'Yes.' He coughs. 'Nick, I wanted to chat about the work you did for the Sheffield branch.'

'Oh, right.'

'I just — look, no one's blaming you. But perhaps it would be an idea to take a little time off. To regroup. What do you think?'

I scratch my chin, puzzled, and realise I've forgotten to shave. And my suit is dirty again, how did that happen? It was clean on today. Or yesterday, maybe. Perhaps Mr Matthews is right, but I can't really take time off just now. There's too much to do, and besides, we could do with saving up a bit of cash.

It's funny how the important things change. You wander through life until you meet that one person and in a moment, you transform; you become *more*. A world forms between you, more real than anything out there; colour, when everything else is grey. You share sentences, thoughts even. You become the breath in each other's lungs.

And then maybe you decide to have kids, and suddenly there's the old cliché — that one of you must go out and provide for your family. And in that moment, you understand your own parents, and their decisions. You understand what it is to have people who depend on you.

It's not easy. I mean, it's relentless. But it defines you. And that's me now. I have a family, I have responsibilities. Jenny's planning to go back to work of course, later on. But for now, it's all up to me. I have to look after them.

So I thank Mr Matthews, and apologise for forgetting to shave, and tell him I'll do better. I don't need the holiday. We'll take it later.

*

Friday.

The others in the office seem a little cheerier today. They're planning drinks. One of them — I can't remember his name — sees me watching them.

'Hey, Nick,' he says. Someone tries to stop him but he shakes her off. 'Do you, ah, want to join us for a pint?'

It's tempting, but I shake my head.

'Thanks, no,' I say. 'I've got to get back to the wife.'

There's a sudden silence in the group, and when I turn back they're all staring at me like I'm from Mars. That's what it's like here. I mean, okay, most of them are quite young, but still, some of them have partners, people they love. Why wouldn't they want to be with them? I shrug.

'Sorry,' I say. 'Next time, maybe.'

I tell Jenny when I get home, and she laughs.

'I've got you totally house-trained,' she says, and then turns back to the TV. I look around.

'Jesus, what a state this place is,' I say. Jenny looks around vaguely.

'Um, yeah. Sorry.'

'Well, yeah, but. I mean ...' *I mean, what the hell do you do all day? I mean ...*

'Never mind,' I say. 'I'll do the washing up.' She doesn't even nod.

The answering machine is blinking. Jenny says, 'Oh, yeah, someone phoned. I left the message on the machine.'

You couldn't even get off the bloody sofa to answer the phone? It's fine. I get the machine. It's a friend of mine, Gordon, asking how I am. Do I want to meet up sometime for a drink? It's always for a drink, down to the pub, out for a laugh. Doesn't anyone stay in anymore? Can't we just have a little, I don't know, domesticity, for god's sake?

What's got into me today?

My suit. I remember my suit. The more I look at it, the dirtier it gets. There are stains all over it. There are stains all, all *fucking* over it.

'I forgot to pick up my clean suit again,' I mutter.

Jenny shrugs. 'Did you hand it in?'

'Yes! Bloody *hell*, we talked about this the other day! Don't you listen?'

She turns around, surprised. 'Why are you angry at me? I'm just saying, isn't your suit in the bedroom?'

'No! I took it to the dry-cleaner's!' I stomp upstairs to the bedroom. My other suit is there, lying in a crumpled heap on the floor, even dirtier than this one.

I don't know how it can be there. I remember taking it to the dry-cleaner's. I'm sure I do. How can it be there? The room is freezing; the suit is cold when I go to pick it up. It feels oily, somehow. I put it down again.

Jenny calls up, 'What about your other suit?'

'Which one?' I say, distracted. I did take it in. I took it in on, what – Tuesday? Last Tuesday?

'The black one?'

'I can't wear that to work, it's a funeral suit. They'll spend the whole day asking if someone's died.'

'Well, you can't wear this one anymore.'

'Fine.' I dig out the black suit from the wardrobe. It's okay, I suppose. At least it's clean. There's something in the pocket, must have been from the last funeral. Whose? Uncle Jack's? It's a small dried flower, with faded blue petals.

When I come back down Jenny is shivering.

'Cold, isn't it?' she asks. I nod. Cold even for November. I turn the gas fire on and the room warms up.

'Bedtime,' she says. I nod again, but suddenly the bedroom is uninviting. It was so cold upstairs. And the suit is still there. I stare at the small flower in my hand.

'We could use the sofa bed tonight, what do you think?' asks Jenny. 'We can cosy up in front of the fire, like we used to in that old flat of yours, remember?'

'Yeah. That was nice.'

'Let's do that. We don't need to go up to the bedroom, we can stay here.'

'Yeah.'

'We don't need to go into the bedroom any more. It's cold there, anyway.'

'Yeah.'

'We can just shut the bedroom door.'

I open the sofa bed and hunt for a sheet. I can only find a couple of old blankets, and Jenny can't remember where the spare duvet is, but that's okay. We huddle up under the blankets and watch the fire, and I listen to Jenny's breathing, so soft over the hiss of the gas, like a whisper in the room.

'She's kicking again,' Jenny murmurs. I put a hand over her belly, that warm stretched skin, and try to feel it.

'Stopped now,' she says.

*

Tuesday.

The bus is quiet today and I have the seat to myself. I'm tired, and I drift in and out of the daze that people adopt to cope with commuter boredom. Every so often I pull out the little dried flower and look at it. I can't remember why I kept it. It's compelling, somehow.

When I get to work, the janitor hasn't opened up yet. I wander around the building, but no one else is in, so I stand under the eaves of the reception area and wait. I slip back into the commuter daze. Sometimes at night I dream the commute: my brain traces the journey over and over again, never letting me go. Sometimes I spend the whole night travelling to work. Now I wait. The sun rises after a while.

It's only as it starts to set again that I wake up with a shock. What time is it? Half-four. How could it be half-four? How could I have spent the whole day here? I can't have. What the hell is going on? My watch must be wrong. But I'm looking at the setting sun, dropping quickly in the November sky.

December, I mean.

Where is everyone? I walk around the building again but there's still no one inside. Is it some holiday I wasn't told about?

I stop for a moment to calm down. I don't know what's happened. It's actually pretty funny that I stood here for so long. It's almost dark now; I shrug and head off home.

When I get back, the TV is off and Jenny is sitting on the sofa staring at the blank screen. Of course it's blank: they cut off the cable because she didn't pay the bill. And the place is an absolute state, dried food and dirty washing and dust everywhere, and why the fuck is she just sitting there?

'You never do *anything!*' I scream. She looks up, gently surprised.

'Hello, Nicky, love,' she says. 'How was your day?'

'Why haven't you done the washing up? Why haven't you tidied? Why am I having to do *everything*? Why couldn't you even pay the fucking *bills*?'

'Well,' she says. 'I was feeling her kick.'

'She never kicks!' I shout. 'She never bloody kicks! You always say she's kicking and she never is, you're lying to me, you're lying!'

I can't understand it, I'm reeling, rage is welling up and I can't control it. I want, oh god, I want to, I could just – I – Oh, *god*.

There's a knock at the door.

I stop shouting and can't remember why I was angry, so I go to answer it. Just before I open the door I think for a weird moment it will be Jenny. But it's not, obviously. It's Gordon.

'Hello, Gordon,' I say.

'Hey, Nick,' he says. He looks sad. He and Donna have been having problems recently, I heard.

'How's things?' I ask cautiously.

'Oh ... fine,' he says. 'How are you doing, mate?'

'Strangest thing,' I say. 'Went to work today, no one else turned up! Must have been a holiday or something, I dunno.'

Gordon frowns. 'It's Saturday,' he says.

'Oh,' I say. 'Well, that would explain it.' Saturday, huh. That would explain it.

'Well, see you,' I say, and start to close the door.

'Hey, Nick!'

I open the door. It's Gordon.

'Hello Gordon,' I say. 'How's things?'

'I – fine.' He stares at me. 'Can I come in for a minute?'

No doubt he wants to talk to me about all about his problems with Donna, but I know Jenny's not up for that.

'Sorry,' I say. 'Jenny's not feeling very well just now.'

He looks shocked.

'What?'

'Sorry, you know how it is.'

'But, Nick. I mean — Jenny? Is that a joke?'

'What?'

'Nick ...' He looks miserable. Must be having a hard time. 'Are you okay?'

I can hear the telly on loud. She does that sometimes when Gordon comes around. I think, actually, she doesn't like Gordon very much.

'I'm fine,' I say. 'Jenny's just not feeling too good. Morning sickness, eh?' I close the door and turn away. Someone behind me knocks loudly, but I ignore it. I head to the sitting room and the sound of the TV. The hall carpet is absolutely covered in little blue petals. Where do they all come from?

When I enter the sitting room, the TV is off. Yes, of course it's off. It's off because she didn't pay the bills. It was always her job to pay the bills. She's looking at me, with her face so beautiful like that, caught in the orange glow from the lights off the street; the only light in the room.

'Feel her kick,' she says.

'She never kicks,' I murmur. 'And it's a boy, anyway.'

'Might be a girl.'

'No. It was a — it's a boy.' I feel like I'm looking at her for the last time, every time. I think the study door is open, behind me. If I turned around, I would see. I would see in.

'Jenny,' I ask, hesitantly. 'How old is it?'

'What?'

'The baby. How old is the baby?'

'Well, she's about five months, Nicky. Have you had a bad day? Come here.'

It's all wrong. 'How can she be five months old?' I shout. 'That's the same as before! She can't be five months! She never kicks! How can you be here? You were in the study! I found you in the *study*! She never kicks!' Someone is hammering on the front door. Jenny looks at me with her face sad and her hair back down again, and her soft lips parted and her beautiful eyes, so blue, like flower petals ...

'Oh, my poor Nicky,' she murmurs. 'Come here. Here, she's kicking now. You can feel her. You can hear her heart, it's here, she's here, come here.' I stare at her. I'm so angry with her. I'm so tired, I've been doing everything myself for so long now, and every time I come home she's there, just sitting there, and I want to — I just want to ... stop.

'Oh, god, Jenny. I'm sorry,' I say, and it's as if all the air has left me, as if all that remains is an empty crumpled black suit. I stumble over to the sofa bed and collapse with my head resting on her belly and she strokes my head. I can hear the banging on the front door but I can feel the baby kicking too, her kicks are in time with the banging, and when I hear her I start to cry.

'She's kicking,' I sob. Jenny laughs.

'Of course she is, you big dafty,' she says. 'You don't have to worry, my love. She's right here at home, all the time, we both are. We're right here. You're looking after us. It's okay. It's okay.'

I breathe out a long, rattling sigh, and lie there until I fall asleep. When I wake up, it's time to go to work.

Here's Guy Russell to close this volume with a reminder that sometimes when you come to the end of the road, you find it isn't the end at all ...

The Haunted Bookshop

Guy Russell

The first time it happened was on a summer afternoon, just after closing, as I was coming in from the storeroom at the back. An elderly man wearing a tweed jacket was sitting in the armchair by the corner bookstacks near the front door. Reading. Solid-looking, not transparent or remotely diaphanous, though haloed by the sun. My first thought was: I'm sure I locked the door. My second was: a customer!

'I'm afraid we're about to close,' I said. 'But can I help you with anything?'

No reply. I remember noticing his book: *Secrets of the Pyramids*. Then I was distracted by a buzzing, tapping sound — a large fly hitting the window — and when I looked back, there was no one there. I looked at the frayed tufting of the armchair. I looked around me. The shop was light and calm and empty. I just saw a ghost, I thought. So they are real. Whatever 'real' means. I touched the armchair, as if worried that it might disappear as well.

'I saw a ghost,' I told Mel that night. 'In the bookshop.'

'It's the sort of place that'd have one,' she said. 'All those creaking stairs and Gothic hidey-holes. All those books on the occult. Probably bodies under the floorboards. Probably used to be a morgue.'

'It's Victorian Gothic. And it was a haberdashers before it was a bookshop. There's no bad feeling about it. It's peaceful.'

And I wasn't scared; more worried by the way that seeing the ghost had disturbed my sense of normality. If something *that* weird could happen, well, anything could.

A few days later, I saw it again. Early afternoon. Sunny. Shop empty, as ever. Same armchair, same tweed jacket, wispy grey hair, wire-rimmed glasses, blue tie. Reading a Stephen King. This time I didn't speak. I looked away with slow deliberation, looked back, and it was still there. I looked away again, looked back, and it – *he* – was gone.

Over the next few weeks, the manifestations – I'd started reading up on the terminology – kept occurring. Any day, any hour, any weather. Once browsing the racks upstairs. Once beside the to-be-sorted pile. Otherwise always in the armchair, reading; though the books varied. *The Mayan Book of the Dead*. Then *The Dumas Club*. Then *Dreams and Astral Projection*, then *The Call of Cthulhu* ...

After a while I lost the sense of surprise, but not of amazement.

'You know like when herons first appeared on the lake,' I said to Mel, 'years ago? Whereas nowadays they're still awesome, but you've got used to what you're seeing?'

'Herons,' she said, 'have a rational explanation.'

All of the next Saturday she sat with me, hoping to see him too. Around lunchtime she went off to the bathroom, and he appeared. She came back, and he was gone.

'How's the bookshop?' our friends would ask me. Many of them were Mel's colleagues from her internet marketing job. They found me amusingly retro, dealing with physical objects. Paper, that twentieth-century material. Rather odd then, that my world of pre-web solidity, compared to theirs of spectral pixels and magic screens, should find itself in the domain of the supernatural.

'It's haunted,' Mel told them.

'Oh, no!' said Elise.

'It's okay. It's an old man who sits in an armchair.'

'He's not scary or threatening,' I said, 'he just appears.'

'Sounds cool,' said Robert. 'Can we see him?'

'I've never seen him,' said Mel. 'Nor has anyone else. He only appears to Jake, when the shop's empty.'

'Da-der da-der da-der,' sang Elsie dramatically.

'It's empty most of the time,' I said. 'Lack of footfall is my big worry. I'm not going to survive on internet orders.'

'But your ghost,' said Robert. 'It's got marketing written all over it.'

'Except he just reads,' I said.

'Hmmm,' said Elise. 'Can't you get it to howl, or something?'

*

'Robert's got a point, you know,' Mel said, when we were in bed that night. I was reading; she was on her Surface Pro. 'You remember you were thinking of renaming the shop? Call it The Haunted Bookshop. Then you'll get footfall. Who can resist a haunted bookshop?'

Certainly something needed to be done. It was Mel's income these days keeping the household afloat. When we'd met, I was in IT, which paid fabulously, but a life spent upgrading finance servers ... Basically, a couple of years ago, I was diagnosed with depression, and we talked about it, and kept trying options, and Mel finally asked, 'Jake – what do you really want to do?'

I felt a twinge of embarrassment, but suppressed it. 'I've always wanted to run a bookshop,' I said.

And Mel thought it was bananas – to her mind, bookshops were mausoleums for a dead commodity – but with typical generosity she went with it. We cut our expenses, and I'd received a small legacy, and the Grove Street second-hand bookshop was for sale. I'd never actually been in there myself, oddly enough: in those days I bought books new, over the internet. The shop was being sold with the stock and furnishings. The former owner had retired suddenly to Lanzarote, where his elder daughter lived.

Well, it *was* bananas. I had no experience in retail. My business plan was a sheet of A4. There was major competition from the High Street charity shops. Overheads were scary. Sales were wryly amusing. Yet despite it all, I was vastly happier. I spent whole afternoons reading in the armchair, almost without guilt, persuading myself I was at work. The chair, incidentally, had come with the shop. It was perfectly positioned to oversee both the desk and the door. I hadn't even moved it.

The next weekend, Robert and Elise came over to the shop. Robert set up a camera with a mic, motion detector, and heat sensor. 'It's like wildlife photography,' he said after four and a half hours. 'It's about patience, and focus. It's like fishing.' Ghosts, as everyone knew, were the otherworldly equivalent of snow leopards: shy creatures, hard to spot, challenging to track, almost impossible to entrap even digitally.

'I think Jake's making it up,' smiled Mel, after the third failure.

'All that reading is giving him visions,' said Robert.

'Are you sure you're all right in the head?' Elise asked me, which actually caused a ghost — the ghost of my former troubles — to appear unexpectedly among us. We exorcised it speedily with laughter.

I emailed Edward, the former owner, to ask if he'd ever seen it, but got no reply. I asked Ivy, one of my few regular customers. She was a crime reader with a crime reader's voraciousness for whole series, and with a habit that even the library and charity shops couldn't assuage.

'Not that I've heard of, dear,' she said. 'The way you describe this thing, it sounds a bit like Edward himself. But he's still alive: I had a letter from him last week. So it can't be *his* ghost.'

Edward had been ill during the purchase process, and I'd only dealt with his younger daughter. It was the illness, Ivy told me, that had caused him to give up the shop and emigrate. 'And the finances, dear, frankly,' she added.

'Mmm, the finances,' I said.

'Anyhow, not any haunting. And he's quite well now.'

'Perhaps he can astrally project,' I smiled. 'Why do we think of ghosts as always being of the dead?'

Ivy gathered her latest basketful of James Pattersons. 'I don't think he would do that kind of thing,' she said.

*

So far I'd left the bookshop pretty much unchanged. To be honest, I liked it as it was, in its labyrinthine oddness: the undiscovered nooks, the extra stairways, the semi-hidden doors to unexpected sanctums. The breadth and idiosyncrasy of the stock, including that huge range of esoterica and occultism that Mel had mentioned. There was even a small section called 'Cosy Horror', a genre I'd never heard of before.

But I did get one thing done: the men came to replace the shopfront sign. 'The Haunted Bookshop,' it now said, not in drips-and-claws Halloween font, but matter-of-factly, in Bookman Old. Once they left, I admired it contentedly, then sat back inside at the desk and went online to check internet orders. Ten minutes later, the door opened. The first customer, I thought, for the renamed shop! I saw the back of a tweed jacket as he closed the door behind him.

Then he turned.

The wispy grey hair, the wire-rimmed glasses, the blue tie —

'Good morning!' he said. 'You look like you've seen a ghost.'

He was less pale than the simulacrum in the armchair, but marginally frailer. His voice had that precise, leisured drawl of the educated older generation.

He was on a brief trip back, he told me, from Lanzarote, and had been keen to come in and see the old place. 'The Canaries are very pleasant, of course,' he said wistfully. 'The sunshine, and so on ... And I had to let the business go. My health — and the finances ...'

'Mmm, the finances,' I said. I told him nonetheless how much I liked the shop, while thinking: so what had I seen all those times? If not him, who?

He accepted a cup of tea, and when I brought it through to him, I found him rather unnervingly ensconced in the armchair, looking at an MR James first edition from a nearby shelf.

'It's like the old days,' he said. 'This was always my favourite spot.'

'I sit there too,' I said, 'when the shop's quiet. As it often is.'

'I was terribly afraid it would become a —' he paused as if noticing a bad odour. 'A tattooists, or something. But you haven't altered it at all.'

This was my chance to ask. 'Except —'

'Except you've put up a new name,' he said, and paused politely. 'It's a surprising one.'

'When you first came in,' I took a breath, 'what made me look shocked, was that ... that I've seen you sitting there, in that chair. Or thought I had,' I backtracked. 'I thought it was a ghost. Hence the new name.'

'I've been haunting the bookshop?' he said, raising an eyebrow and regarding me for a moment with a cryptic smile, as if he thought I was mad. 'Or perhaps it's my twin brother. He died on this very spot, you know. After being hideously clubbed to death with a large volume of the *Britannica* ... Only joking.' He waved the book humorously. 'Too much of this stuff.'

'And you only appear to me.'

'How selfish. And then you doubt your sanity. That's how the genre goes. Do you hear voices?'

'You don't speak,' I said. 'You just read.'

'What sort of thing?'

'Lovecraft. Stephen King. Magic and the occult.'

'Well, it does sound like me.'

'Anyway, there was some kind of presence. And we thought the name change might help with the finances.'

'I can see that,' he looked thoughtful. 'Especially if you have a real ghost.'

The shop door went again. I stood up. It was Mel. 'Guess what?' I said to her. 'Edward's here! Edward, who owned this place before —'

I turned round to the armchair.

The seat. The back.

The frayed tufting.

No!

It couldn't be, I decided, as the shock began to recede. Ghosts didn't hold conversations, did they? He'd said, 'You look like you've seen a ghost.' Ghosts weren't witty, were they? They didn't have a sense of humour. Surely?

I sat back in the desk chair and put my head in my hands. The untouched cup of tea was still beside one of the chair legs, steaming innocently.

'He was there!' I said. 'We were speaking, like live, real, normal, living humans ... No. There's something really wrong with me, Mel. This isn't depression. Not this time. This is something worse.'

She put her arms around me, as if to assure me she was real.

'I saw him,' said Mel. 'Through the door. I saw him in the chair.'

*

Three days later, I was in the armchair reading a book called *Shamanic Magic* and so engrossed that when the door went, it was an effort for me to wrench myself back to the real world.

It was Ivy.

'That gave me a shock, dear. I thought you were Edward there!'

'It's the best place to sit.'

'That's what he used to say.'

'Well, it's true.' I got up and went to the desk. 'Can I help you?'

'I've some news, dear, first,' and as she spoke, I already knew. 'His daughter emailed,' Ivy told me. 'Out there in hospital, it was. Peaceful. I've sent condolences.'

'Three days ago,' I said.

'Oh! You knew already!'

I shook my head. It was becoming clear: he had been passing through. 'I sort of guessed.'

Having delivered her important news, Ivy went into the next room, and in due time returned to the desk with an armful of Maigrets. I was counting them when I saw something was wrong. She was looking across the room.

'Oh,' she said, and stopped. 'Edward! Oh. He ... there in the chair. That time it *was* him! Oh.'

I sat her down in the desk chair. 'Well I never,' she said.

A few days later, a couple of Goth kids came in, perhaps lured by the new name, and were rewarded with a manifestation. Word went round quickly after that. Even Robert and Elise had one – on the one time Robert didn't have his camera. A local reporter did a piece, which helped, though the ghost avoided her. Many of the new visitors bought books, and when a local exorcist offered his services, I told him certainly not.

We were visited by a medium, who sat in the armchair and declared she felt 'presence within', and that 'the energy was strong' in the horsehair stuffing. Yet who was I to scoff? I was getting well into the shop's extensive sections on the occult.

I made one more change: I got a second armchair, and put it beside the first – for when I had time to use it. Our Halloween event was jammed with customers. Likewise our Christmas ghost-story reading, at which I thought for a moment I saw him – it was very much his thing, after all – but it may have been the candlelight.

At quiet times though, he's frequently there in the old armchair. Something might intrude deep in my reading, and I'll take my glasses off, pass my hand through my own greying hair, and look over. But he's never looked at me again, let alone spoken. He's always too busy, too rapt; his head down, transported within his armchair to haunt some fantastical place. Sometimes wide-eyed, sometimes smiling, always book in hand, he looks as if he couldn't be more content. As if the bookshop were his manifestation of Heaven. As if eternity, for him, is the perfect opportunity to get more reading done.

About the Contributors

Alastair Chisholm writes short stories and children's books. His first children's picture book – *The Prince and the Witch and the Thief and the Bears* – was published in 2018 by Walker Books.

He lives in Edinburgh with his wife, two children, and a cat, and he finds it very odd to refer to himself in the third person. He likes biscuits.

You can read more about him at www.alastairc.com, or follow him on Twitter at @alastair_ch.

Alex Clark's short stories have appeared in various print publications and online journals, including *Prole, Litro Online, MIR Online, Shooter Literary Magazine,* and anthologies by The Fiction Desk. She lives in Cheltenham, where she runs the quarterly live flash fiction night Flashers' Club.

You can find her tweeting at @otheralexclark, and read her blog at theotheralexclark.wordpress.com.

Lahra Crowe studied literature at the University of Glasgow and later went on to complete a PGDE in English at The University of Edinburgh. Having lived in Scotland all of her life, she and her husband decided to embark on new adventures in 2016, moving first to Chicago, then later to Switzerland, where they currently reside. Lahra loves art, politics, and literature and has often thought about writing creatively in her spare time, however it has only been recently that she has started to experiment. Winning The Fiction Desk's Newcomer Prize has definitely encouraged her to continue.

Matt Harris is a writer from Liverpool whose poetry and short fiction have previously appeared in *HOAX*, *Confingo*, the *Alarmist*, the *Nottingham Review*, and others. His website is horridwithcogs.wordpress.com.

Michael Hurst grew up in Essex and now lives in Cheltenham with his wife and daughter. As well as writing, he enjoys taking photos, playing the piano, and walking in the Cotswold countryside. He was shortlisted for the 2018 Newcomer Prize and hopes to finish his first novel this year. You can find him on Twitter at @CotswoldArts.

Guy Russell was born in Chatham and has been a holiday courier, purchasing clerk, media analyst, and fan-heater production operative. He now lives in Milton Keynes. Work in *Madame Morte* (Black Shuck), *Brace* (Comma), *Troubles Swapped For Something Fresh* (Salt), *The Iron Book of New Humorous Verse* (Iron), and elsewhere. He sometimes reviews poetry for *Tears in the Fence*.

Poppy Toland is a London-based editor and literary translator. She has translated four novels, two novellas, and a number of short stories from Chinese. 'Our Gaff' won second place in the Fiction Desk's Newcomer Prize and is the first of her own stories to be published.

For more information on the contributors
to this volume, please visit our website:

www.thefictiondesk.com/authors

Also Available

the first twelve Fiction Desk anthologies:

www.thefictiondesk.com